Emily Harvale

Tasty Treats at Seahorse Bites Café

To my fantastic friends, David, Kitty, Rachel, Jeanette, Eileen, Susan and Luke, who all helped to keep me sane and smiling during my recent move to my wonderful new home. Moving home 3 days before Christmas, during a lockdown, in a pandemic, is not a lot of fun – but you all made me laugh and reminded me to look to the future. I love you all. Thank you for being my friends. xxx

Map of Seahorse Harbour

There's an interactive map, with more details, on my website: www.emilyharvale.com

One

'I blame Nathan Bromley.'

Asher sipped his coffee and looked at me over the rim of his mug as if he thought I'd gone completely mad. Mind you, over the years my brother has often given me that same look, so it wasn't really a surprise. The look that said he wished he had a normal sister. One who didn't keep getting herself into awkward – or downright awful situations, many of which, he seemed compelled to help resolve, thankfully.

And I must admit, he has got me out of some very bad situations.

One was a disastrous marriage to an extremely handsome man, who turned out to be a pig. No. That's not fair to pigs. The man was a complete and utter bastard. I can't even bring myself to mention his name.

I was young at the time. Everyone, except me, had reservations about the marriage. But I was in love, and I wouldn't listen to common sense or reason.

Sadly, I still don't.

Yet even after all these years, I sometimes wake up in a cold sweat in the middle of the night, having had a nightmare that I'm still living under his control. Thanks to Asher, I'm not. My short-lived time as a wife involved several dramas of biblical proportions. Disastrous is actually an understatement. In fact, if it hadn't been for Asher, I might not be here today.

With yet another broken heart.

Well, not another heart exactly. I only have the one, obviously. But it's been broken so many times since it first beat out my arrival into the world, thirty-three years, five months and six days ago, that I'm amazed it keeps managing to fix itself.

You might assume that, having had such a nightmare of a marriage, I would be wary of falling in love.

You'd be wrong.

If anything, I think it's had the opposite effect. I seem to fall in love at the drop of a hat. I can't stop myself. And over the years I have tried, believe me.

The thing is, I'm an eternal optimist where Love is concerned. No matter how many times my heart takes a battering, I get back in the dating ring and slug it out once more, in the hope of finding my One True Love.

He's out there. Somewhere. I know he is.

'Nathan?' Even Lottie, the love of my brother's life – whom he met at Christmas, just two short months ago – looked sceptical. She glanced from me to Asher, as she tucked a wayward strand of strawberry blonde hair behind her left ear. 'What does Nathan have to do with it?'

Asher shrugged and I sighed dramatically.

'Everything! It's all his fault.'

'Er. How, exactly?' Asher raised one brow and gave me another of his looks.

'Because he told me that if I were *his* girlfriend, there was no way he'd leave me alone on Valentine's Day, especially not as it was the weekend. Not even if his career depended on it. And then asked why Sean had to work the entire weekend anyway because none of the accountants he knew ever did that. Not that Sean is an accountant. He's a financial advisor. Which shows how much Nathan knows. I never should've listened to him. And then he said that he was sure Sean must have something special planned for me and would surprise me by either arriving at the Valentine's dance, albeit late, or would turn up on the actual day with an apology and enough flowers to fill Kew Gardens. Twice.'

I saw the look pass between Asher and Lottie.

'I still don't see how–'

'Oh bloody hell, Ash.' I only call him Ash

when I'm cross because I know he doesn't really like it. 'Sean didn't turn up, did he?'

'N-o.'

'Precisely. So I started having doubts. Just because of the things bloody Nathan, bloody Bromley said. And I asked Sean why he'd had to work all of Valentine's weekend. He got annoyed and said we couldn't all swan around doing whatever we liked, whenever we liked. Which wasn't totally fair. Because I don't swan around. I work very hard. Most of the time. But when I pointed that out, Sean got the hump. And when I asked why he hadn't answered any of my calls, he said that I shouldn't be calling him fifteen times in two hours, especially as he'd told me he'd be working.'

'He had a point. Fifteen calls was a rather excessive number. Except he wasn't working.'

I hate it when Asher states the obvious. I love my brother to bits, but sometimes he can be a right pain in the arse. Then again, so can I. That's the one thing Asher and I have in common. That and our looks. Although I'm not as tall, nor as solidly built as he is. I'm a good three inches shorter and the only definition my muscles have is hidden beneath my skin. I do have the same treacle-coloured hair and skin just a few shades lighter. But my skin is a smidgeon fairer than his. Mainly because, unlike him, I don't go out running two or three times a day. In fact, I never go out running. A leisurely stroll is enough exercise for me.

Although since Asher's been with Lottie, I hear he runs a lot less. At least that's what Lilith Shoe told me at the Valentine's dance. And her word is gospel in Seahorse Harbour. She owns the Sunrise B&B in Rock Road, up on Seahorse Cliffs and she's the local gossip. What Lilith doesn't know isn't worth knowing.

I'm also not quite as good-looking as my brother. Although I have to say, he doesn't look his best right now. His usually clean-shaven jaw is looking a bit stubbly. His eyes are sleepy. Even his voice isn't as firm and commanding. But then it is a Sunday, and he and Lottie have clearly just got out of bed. They weren't exactly expecting me today, especially as I'd spent almost an hour last night crying down the phone to them and telling them Sean and I were over.

But where else could I go? Since my marriage break-up seven years ago, I'm back living with Mum and Dad and I couldn't stay there today. They're lovely people, but when I'm going through a heartbreak, they're not really the most understanding. I always head for Asher's at times like these. And there seem to be rather a lot of them.

I wish Asher didn't live so far away. But the moment he set foot in Seahorse Harbour we all knew he'd end up living here. We first came here on a family holiday during the last two weeks of August in 1998 when Asher was sixteen and I was nearly twelve. He's thirty-eight now and I'm nearly thirty-four. He found an injured seagull with a broken wing and took it to the village vet, Barney Short. Short is also Lottie's surname but they're not related. Asher and Barney got on like a house on fire and Asher spent the rest of his holiday at Barney's surgery, helping out. That's when he decided he would be a vet, and he moved here as soon as he could, eventually taking over the practice when Barney retired.

Asher loves this place and has become a real part of the community. He's also a Seahorse Rider. They're all volunteers who help look after the seahorses who live in an area called The Shallows, in the bay at the foot of Seahorse Cliffs, right near a particularly quirky sight-seeing spot called The Weeping Eye. I'll tell you about that later.

The Seahorse Riders monitor the seagrass and the water. They keep the beaches clean and encourage everyone else to do likewise. They actually organise beach clean-ups in Seahorse Harbour. I've been to several over the years and they're really good fun.

The Seahorse Riders also deter would-be seahorse hunters who might try to take the seahorses for pets or souvenirs, and they raise awareness of the plight of the cute little creatures, along with funds to help save them.

There are more than fifty species of seahorses worldwide, so Asher says, but even so, many of them are classed as vulnerable and a few are now on the endangered list. That's not just because of hunters. They suffer due to pollution and to boats churning up the grasses in which they live.

The two species found in UK waters are called the Spiny Seahorse and the Short Snouted Seahorse, and thankfully both were granted protected status back in 2008. They're still at risk though, but The Seahorse Riders do a sterling job.

Seahorse Harbour is home to the Spiny Seahorse, and as I said, they live in an area called The Shallows, but they do move into deeper water when the weather gets really bad. The Shallows is at the foot of the cliffs and has cliffs on three sides, so the water tends to get rather rough down there at times.

The Seahorse Riders' offices are based in a small sea life centre on Sea Walk, just around the cliffs to one side of The Shallows. The centre is called Seahorse Tales and children from nearby schools can visit to learn about the seahorses and other marine life.

That's where Asher used to spend most of his time when he wasn't in his surgery, or on the water, or running to keep fit, or in the local pub, The Seahorse Inn, which is owned by his friend, Mikkel Meloy. Mikkel is originally from

Norway and I have to say, he's bloody gorgeous. Imagine Chris Hemsworth. Only blonder and more Viking-looking.

I could easily have fallen in love with Mikkel. Actually, I think I did. But it was obvious that he saw me as his friend's little sister and nothing else, and I don't believe in wasting time.

Which is something else Asher and I have in common. Although Asher doesn't fall in love anywhere near as often as I do. He did fall for Josie Parnell last summer, but Lilith told me it was clear from the start who she would end up with.

Josie had come to the village to visit her twin sister, Diana, and also their aunt, Elsie. Diana and her husband Alex Dunn, own a really posh holiday home at the top of Church Hill, but since last summer, Diana and their two kids have been living there on an almost permanent basis while Alex remained in London. Elsie owns a beautiful cottage just a few steps from the promenade, with glorious views of the bay.

Asher also fell for Lottie the minute he saw her staring into a shop window on Church Row the night she arrived.

But prior to falling for Josie and Lottie, Asher's hardly been in love at all. Unlike me.

Now he spends most of his free time with Lottie and her gorgeous, black and white springer spaniel, Merry. Lottie's learning all about the seahorses and although she's only been in the village since the week before Christmas, she's also quickly become a part of the community. It's obvious, even to me, that she adores the seahorses as much as she adores Asher.

Who was clearly waiting for me to respond to his barb about Sean.

'I realise that,' I said. 'But at the time I thought he was. Except Nathan made me think that Sean had some big surprise for me. Which he did, of course. But not the sort of surprise I was expecting.'

I swear I saw a flicker of a grin on Asher's face, but he rapidly replaced it with a frown.

'Let me get this straight. You're blaming Nathan for planting doubts about Sean. Doubts that made you ask questions.' He shot a look at Lottie, shaking his head slightly. 'And then search your boyfriend's briefcase, suit pockets, and finally his wallet, where you found a receipt for a hotel room for Valentine's weekend. And when Sean eventually admitted he spent the weekend with a girl from his office and couldn't decide whether he wanted to stay with you, or dump you and be with her, that is somehow Nathan's fault?'

'Yes.'

Asher let out a breath of exasperation. Another thing he often does when talking to me.

'You can hardly blame Nathan for that, Sorcha. As a matter of fact, I think you should be thanking him. If he hadn't sown those seeds of doubt, you wouldn't have asked those questions or searched Sean's things. It might've been weeks before you discovered Sean was seeing someone else.'

'Yes. And we'd still be together and I wouldn't be heartbroken and he might've decided it was me he wanted to be with, after all. And not some twenty-year-old bimbo.'

'Why would you want to be with a man like that? Especially one you've only been dating since New Year's Eve!'

Asher looked genuinely astonished.

'Because I loved him. I'm pretty sure I did. And for your information it's been longer than that. We've been dating since the beginning of November.'

'November?' Shock, and perhaps a flash of anger, swept across Asher's face. 'Why didn't you tell me?'

'Because I knew what you'd say. And besides, it's better to be with someone than to be alone.'

Asher tutted. 'No, it's not.'

'Actually,' Lottie said, her fingers brushing against Asher's arm. 'Sometimes it is. Or it seems as if it is. Some of us don't relish being alone.'

His eyes filled with love and tenderness and even I could feel the warmth of his smile as he took her fingers in his and squeezed them.

'You'll never be alone again, Lottie. You have me now. And you always will. And not just me, of course. You have your mum. And Josie and Diana. And all your new friends here in Seahorse Harbour. Sorcha's never been alone. She's always had me and Mum and Dad.' He dragged his gaze from Lottie and showered me with some of that affection. 'Do you ... do you feel alone, Sorcha? If so, you should've said something before. We could work on that. Is that why you keep falling in love – with all the wrong people?'

'I don't keep...'

I stopped mid-sentence. I couldn't really deny it. I do keep falling in love. And yes. With all the wrong people. I think it's a fault in my genes.

I shook my head and sighed. He would never understand. I'm not really sure I understood, myself. He was right. I did have him, and Mum and Dad. They all loved me. I knew that. But it wasn't the same.

It may be daft. Or even a bit pathetic, but all I've ever wanted is to be in love. To share my life with someone special. To be part of an inseparable couple. I'd had that briefly, but instead of the fairy tale, I got a nightmare.

It didn't put me off though. I want my

knight in shining armour. My Prince Charming. I know we're not supposed to admit that these days. We women are all supposed to be career-driven. Successful. Independent. Self-supporting. But that's just not me.

I want to be a wife and a mother. I want to take care of the man I love. I've never wanted a career. Unlike Asher, I never had a vocation. I've tried to pretend to be someone else, but I always fail miserably. Is it so wrong to say I want to be a stay-at-home-mum? I want a husband and I want a family of my own.

I'm not lazy, believe me. And being a wife and mother is hard work. I've seen that with my friends. I just want a future with one man who loves me. And only me. Is that too much to ask?

And yes. I do fall in love a lot. And I've already admitted it's with all the wrong men. But is that really my fault?

I came to visit Asher at Halloween last year and met a guy who was staying at the Seahorse Harbour Holiday Park. I fell for him in a big way, but he was a bit of a bastard too. He almost conned me into handing over most of my savings. I won't go into details but Asher came to my rescue – again, and the guy did a disappearing act. Thankfully, without my money.

My brother's very protective of me. And of my money. I'm not loaded, by any means, but an aunt of ours left us both a tidy sum when we were in our twenties. Asher used his to buy Barney's cottage, which is where he lives now. Part of it houses the veterinary practice, so it made total sense. I put mine in my bank account, where it's been slowly dwindling. Although if Asher hadn't stepped in when he did at Halloween, I might've lost the lot. I thought I was going to double my money in six months. It turned out the only person who'd be doubling their money was the bloody conman who'd convinced me we were soulmates.

Okay. I *am* an idiot.

Why do I keep falling for these people?

But that's how I met Sean.

Asher told me I should get my finances sorted out. He was amazed I hadn't done so already. He offered to help, of course, but I decided it was something I could do on my own. And just to prove I could, I immediately found myself a financial advisor, via a friend of a friend.

Sean and I hit it off from the get-go, and although he said he shouldn't become romantically involved with a client, it was pretty obvious from the second I walked into his office, that he would. Within just a few hours of us meeting, Sean was handling a lot more than my finances.

I didn't tell Asher, or anyone else about Sean for a while. And even then, I hate to admit this, but I lied. I said we'd met at a New Year's

Eve party. Well, I knew what they'd all say if I told them the truth. That I'd fallen for Sean just one week after the Halloween debacle. Mum and Dad – and Asher – made it clear they thought I should stay away from men for a time. But what can I say? I'm a passionate person. I do have a tendency to fall in love pretty fast, but I can't help myself. I really can't.

Which is why I was at Asher's cottage, my heart broken once again.

I probably should've asked if I could come and stay, during our conversation of the previous night. But I had never asked before so it didn't occur to me. I'd often turn up on Asher's doorstep and he'd always welcome me with open arms, so I didn't hesitate this time.

But Asher's never been in a serious relationship before. I'd obviously got them out of bed. When Asher had opened the front door in just a dressing gown, I thought he must be ill, until I heard Lottie's dog Merry, bark and I realised Lottie was there.

I should've thought of that. They'd been practically living together since Christmas. But when your heart is breaking, common sense and reason aren't top of the agenda.

I'd offered to go and have a coffee somewhere and come back later – which was a pretty stupid thing to say, even for me. The only place open that early on a Sunday morning was Seahorse Bites Café. I wouldn't have gone there. Not if you'd paid me. Nathan Bromley was the last person I wanted to see today. Or any day.

I could picture Nathan's face if I'd walked into the café. He'd know immediately what had happened. He seemed to have a sixth sense about stuff like that. Lyn, his aunt is the same. She can sniff out relationship problems from a mile away. Or any other problems. Unlike Lyn, Nathan doesn't have the tact or diplomacy to deal with it. Lyn is like a sort of cuddly aunt. Nathan is like ... the complete opposite of that.

He definitely isn't cuddly. I've seen him in his swim shorts several times, and his body is as solid as the rocks in the bay. His hair's the colour of sand, unlike Lyn's. Hers is a mass of tight blonde curls. The sort you'd see on a child. Or a Fairy Godmother in the movies. She has a cheerful smile, rosy cheeks, soft, warm blue eyes and a gentle, soothing voice.

Nathan's eyes are intense. Sometimes they appear to be green and sometimes they're grey but whatever colour they are, when he looks at me, I completely forget what I'm saying because his eyes seem to be boring into me. And his voice, like his jaw, is firm and rather intimidating. He's got well defined cheek bones and a long, aquiline nose and he gives me the impression that he's looking down on me. Or telling me off. Neither of which he has any right to do. It's not as if I know him that well. Not really.

I've seen him a few times over the years when I've been staying with Asher and Nathan's been staying with his aunt. We always chat and pass the time of day. But he's not really my type. He's too serious. And he's a real goody two-shoes, as my mum would say. I don't think the guy has ever been in any sort of trouble in his life.

Now he's moved to Seahorse Harbour and is working with Lyn at Seahorse Bites Café. She's been running the place on her own since her husband died, so she must be relieved to have some help. But I suppose it means I'll be seeing more of Nathan, whether I like it or not.

He certainly made his presence felt at the Valentine's dance last weekend. And he was definitely the catalyst for the break-up of my relationship, no matter what Asher and Lottie say.

In future I'll tell him to keep his advice and his opinions to himself. His aunt Lyn loves to give people advice, so I assume he gets that from her, but Lyn's also incredibly kind and generous and she does a lot of work for several charities, including Asher's beloved, 'Save the Seahorse' campaign.

I'm not sure what Nathan does. Apart from swagger about the place giving unwanted advice. Although Lyn says he's a better cook than she is – which is pretty awesome, because

Lyn's food is great. It's nothing fancy. Just home cooked, wholesome meals, but they taste almost as divine as the cordon bleu dishes in Mikkel Meloy's restaurant, Hippocampus, and they definitely equal anything Mikkel serves up in his pub, The Seahorse Inn.

Lottie, Josie and Diana, who are all around my age, think Nathan's "hiding his light under a bushel". But I can't really see it.

Actually, come to think of it, it was Elsie who said he was hiding something. And she should know about how to hide things. She kept one hell of a secret until last Christmas. Elsie's in her sixties, but she definitely doesn't act her age. But none of that has anything to do with this. Lottie, Josie and Diana all just said the guy is hot. And that I *definitely* don't see.

I must admit he did look a little cute last Saturday morning when Josie teased him by saying he was a very tasty treat in Lyn's bright yellow apron, which he'd borrowed after I spilled a glass of orange juice down the front of his white shirt. She added that he'd look even better in just the apron, and the guy turned the colour of blood. He blushed from top to toe, I swear, and for one brief moment, when he shot a look at me, something flipped inside my tummy. But that might've been because I'd just eaten a huge, cooked breakfast, followed by a chocolate muffin.

Diana told Josie off for flirting. As if she

hasn't done enough of that herself recently, from what I hear. Josie laughed and said it was harmless fun, which I'm sure it was. Everyone knows she adores her partner, Liam, and also Liam's teenaged-daughter, Orla. But she does have a wicked sense of humour.

You'd never guess Josie and Diana are twins. They do look a little alike, but Diana is graceful and serene and appears to be a domestic goddess. Even her hair is perfect. It's the colour of dark, golden honey and it sort of shimmers as it moves. Josie's hair is almost back to its natural colour of chestnut brown, but the bright red dye hasn't fully grown out yet, and it's rather wild – a bit like Josie once was, some might say. Josie will be the first to admit she's no domestic goddess, but now she's with Liam, she appears to be heading in that direction.

I prefer Josie to Diana, who has a tendency to make you feel as if she's better than you are, somehow. But she does have a drop-dead gorgeous, heart surgeon for a husband, not to mention, he's a millionaire, so I suppose that's why.

Not that her life has been a bed of roses. Alex's hands may be steady in the operating theatre but unfortunately, he's got a wandering eye. I know at least two people he's definitely had an affair with, and apparently, there's a long line of women in his past.

Since Christmas and all the drama that went with it, he's supposed to have completely changed his ways. We'll have to see how long that lasts.

I wasn't here at Christmas. We couldn't get here due to the snow blizzards, but I heard about it from Asher when Mum, Dad and I came to visit him in January. Although as Asher never gossips, he left out all the juicy bits. I heard all those from Lilith at the Valentine's dance last weekend. Which was also when I remembered why I didn't fancy Nathan Bromley in the least.

'Where's your latest boyfriend?' he asked, in a distinctly disapproving tone while those intense eyes of his scanned me from head to foot.

'Latest?' I replied. 'I'm not sure what you mean by that. But at least I have a significant other. I don't see you here with anyone on your arm. Sean's working all weekend otherwise he'd be here.'

He frowned at me. 'Why are you biting my head off? I was only asking.'

'It was the way you asked. You can be rather pompous you know.'

He raised his brows. 'Pompous? Me? You were the one who made the 'significant other' remark. But you're right. I don't have a girlfriend. If I did, I wouldn't work all of Valentine's weekend, that's for definite. Are you sure he's working?'

'What? Of course he is. Why would you even ask that?'

He shrugged and stuffed his hands in the pocket of his black trousers.

'If you were my girlfriend, nothing would get in the way of me spending the entire weekend with you. Perhaps he'll turn up later and surprise you. Or he'll arrive tomorrow with enough flowers to fill Kew Gardens twice over, and spend the whole day making it up to you.'

I stared at him, open-mouthed for a moment or two.

'That's … incredibly romantic. Are you ill? That's not at all like you.'

His eyes met mine and he seemed a bit cross.

'That just goes to show that you don't know me at all. I hope you have a lovely evening, Sorcha. And I really hope that this one doesn't let you down.'

And there it was. Nathan Bromley. A pompous, mean, opinionated git.

Which was why there was no way I could've gone to Seahorse Bites Café this morning, after getting Asher and Lottie out of bed. I would've had to have sat on the bench under the ancient oak tree outside the church, St Mary Star of the Sea, instead. And on a freezing, February morning, that wasn't a good idea.

'Don't be ridiculous,' Asher had thankfully said. Although he did look a little worn out. 'Come in and I'll put the kettle on.'

'Some clothes might be good,' I'd quipped, astonishing myself that I could still make jokes when my heart was shattered into tiny pieces.

Asher gave me a quick grin before asking me what was wrong. Almost as if he'd completely forgotten everything I'd said last night.

'Apart from me having had my heart broken again, you mean?'

I'd tried to put on a brave face as I stepped inside. I'd got them out of bed, I couldn't burst into tears right away. Even if I had wanted to.

Asher hugged me to him. Although he did sigh rather loudly first and shake his head. And I saw him dart a look at Lottie. Almost an apologetic one.

Lottie came to comfort me while Asher went upstairs to dress.

Asher's cottage looks old and rustic on the outside, but inside it isn't at all what you'd expect, especially not as the exterior is painted bright pink. The interior is bang-on-trend and rather sleek and shiny. The kitchen is like one you'd see in a stylish magazine and it's black with red tiles. The sitting room has dark green walls and black leather furniture. The wood is tinted ebony. His home is always pristine – apart from when I come to stay. He says it looks as if a troupe of chimpanzees has had a rave and invited half the jungle after I've been there a day.

He's not wrong.

Which is why I was astonished when I followed Lottie into the kitchen so that she could make some coffee. There were muddy pawprints trailing from the garden to the kitchen door. An equally muddy jacket was slung over the back of one of the designer, kitchen chairs. Dog food had been spilled on the counter and all around the bowl on the tiled floor, where a pool of water circled the water bowl. There were definite claw marks on one of the cupboard doors, which I'm sure weren't there last weekend. Or maybe I hadn't noticed. I do recall Asher telling me that cupboard was where they kept Merry's treats.

As if on cue, Merry came bounding in, with one of those rope toys hanging from her mouth, which she dropped at my feet. I wasn't really in a playful mood, but who can resist a dog? Especially one as cute as Merry. I bent down to pick up the toy but she beat me to it. I gently tussled her for it and in doing so, managed to kick Lottie on her leg.

'Oh God. I'm sorry, Lottie.'

'Don't worry about it.'

She smiled at me as she rubbed her leg. And that's when I saw it.

'Is that...? Bloody hell! Are you and Asher

engaged? When did that happen? You weren't engaged last weekend.'

She flushed crimson and beamed at me, but her happiness was tinged with sadness.

'Last night. Asher would've told you ... but we didn't think it was the right time ... what with...'

She let her voice trail off, but I knew what she meant. What with me phoning to tell them yet another of my relationships had bitten the dust.

God. I can be so selfish sometimes. I'd spent ages last night going on and on about how life wasn't fair, and all that stuff, when, little did I know, they were in the middle of celebrating their engagement.

And earlier this morning, I hadn't spotted the ring and neither of them had mentioned it.

No wonder Asher kept casting odd little glances at Lottie. He was probably wondering how and when they were going to get a chance to tell me.

Asher strolled back into the kitchen right at that moment and darted another of those looks from Lottie to me.

'You're engaged!' I spluttered.

He nodded. 'Yes. Sorry, Sorcha. I was going to tell you.'

'Sorry?' I flung myself at him and hugged him so tight he made a squeak, so I relaxed my hold a little. 'Why should you be sorry? Oh,

Asher. This is wonderful news. I'm thrilled for you!' I let him go and embraced Lottie, taking care not to squeeze her so tightly. 'Congratulations, Lottie. And welcome to the family. I'm so excited I could cry.'

And I did. Although I'm ashamed to say that some of those tears were of self-pity.

I really was delighted for Asher and Lottie. Truly I was. They might not have been together long but everyone could see they were made for one another.

But I couldn't help but wonder why I can never seem to meet the man who was made for me.

Perhaps I've been looking in all the wrong places.

Or, knowing my luck, even though I'm sure there is, perhaps there isn't a man out there who's right for me.

Two

'How long are you planning to stay?' Asher asked during lunch.

We were having roast beef with all the trimmings which all three of us had helped prepare and we'd had so much fun in the kitchen that I'd almost forgotten my heart was broken.

Asher had told Lottie that no one in the world could make Yorkshire puddings like mine, so naturally, I had to make them. I would've helped out anyway, but his praise did lift my spirits, I'll admit. We all need a little bit of that from time to time, don't we? And I certainly needed a boost right then.

Asher has always known how to cheer me up. I suppose that's one of the reasons I invariably turn to him. That and because he's the best brother a girl could have.

He's always been protective of me. From the moment I was introduced to him in the hospital he decided he was going to look after me. Mum and Dad told us – and they still tell everyone they meet, should the opportunity arise – that he actually stood beside the bed as a lanky four-year-old, and when Mum said, "Asher, this is your baby sister, Sorcha Daphne Elizabeth Bryant", Asher gently stroked my head and said, "I'm Asher, your big brother. And I'm not going to let anything bad happen to you. Ever."

Mum said it brought a tear to her eye. Apparently, he'd been reading a comic in which a big brother says something along those lines to his sister. Only that brother was some sort of superhero.

Mind you, Asher is a superhero as far as I'm concerned. He may not always be able to stop bad things happening, but he does try his best. And he's always there to pick up the pieces.

He's never asked me how long I planned to stay before though, so when he did, for one brief moment I wondered if things were going to change now that he and Lottie were engaged.

'Have I outstayed my welcome already?'

I tried to sound light-hearted but I'm not sure that worked because Asher frowned at me.

'Don't be ridiculous. You're always welcome here. You know that.' He glanced at Lottie.

She smiled at him and then at me.

'I think what Asher meant was that last

night, after he proposed, we bounced around some ideas about having a party or something. I'm not very good at arranging things like that, so I said, if we did, I'd definitely need some help. I was going to ask Elsie and of course, Josie and Diana, but if you're going to be here for a while, perhaps you could help too.'

'Exactly.' Asher nodded and blew Lottie a kiss.

My eyes probably bulged out of my head. Asher knows how much I love organising a party.

'Are you serious?' I sounded like a demented banshee, I was sure. Not that I know what a banshee sounds like. Demented or otherwise. But you know what I mean.

Asher and Lottie beamed at one another and in unison, said, 'Absolutely!'

'Oh my God. I'd love to. Yes. Thank you both. This is just what I need. Something wonderful to look forward to. And what could be more wonderful than celebrating my brother getting engaged? Do you have a particular date in mind? Or a venue?'

Asher grinned. 'We didn't really discuss it in detail. It was just an idea I sort of threw out there. We'd been to dinner at Hippocampus, and I'd proposed outside of the shop where we first met.'

'Aww! That's so romantic. Did you go down on one knee? Was the pavement wet? It rained last night. At least it did at home.'

Asher pulled a face. 'Yes, I did. And it was wet but it was worth it.'

'I had no idea he was intending to propose.' Lottie's eyes sparkled with love. 'We'd had a lovely meal and we were walking home when Asher turned towards Church Row. I actually thought he'd had too much to drink and had forgotten the way home.' She laughed merrily.

'I did drink quite a lot of wine,' Asher admitted, beaming at Lottie. 'I don't think I've ever felt so nervous in my life as I did last night. I was pretty sure you would say yes, but a tiny part of me kept wondering if you might think it was too soon. Or you might just say no.'

'Too soon?' Lottie laughed louder. 'I'd have said yes if you'd asked me on Christmas Eve!'

Asher exhaled an exaggerated breath. 'If I'd known that, I probably would've done. I knew the minute I saw you that you were the one for me.'

'I felt the same,' Lottie said.

I felt like a gooseberry. And from the way they were gazing into each other's eyes, I think they possibly forgot I was there for a second or two.

I wouldn't have been surprised if Asher had swept everything from the table, grabbed Lottie and made love to her right then and there.

Thankfully, he didn't.

I gave a small cough and they both looked a little startled as they came back down to earth.

'So, you were telling me about the date and venue.'

'Ah yes. Er. After I proposed and Lottie accepted, we came home and ... Well, you don't need to know that bit.' Asher glanced down at his plate.

'But later,' Lottie said, stepping in instantly. 'We were chatting about when and how we'd tell everyone, and who'd we'd tell first.'

'I hope I was high on that list.'

They both smiled at me.

'You were equal to Mum and Dad.' Asher topped up my wine glass. 'And to Elsie.'

'Excellent. Thank you.' I clinked my glass with his.

'You're welcome.'

We grinned at each other.

'That's when I suggested that perhaps we could have a party or something,' Asher added.

'And I loved the idea, but as I said, I'm not very good at stuff like that. We hadn't got as far as deciding on a date or anything because Asher said I couldn't be good at everything and I was good at all the things that mattered and ... er ... well we...'

'Yes. I get the picture,' I said.

And I did. It was obvious they'd spent most

of last night having sex. Conversation clearly hadn't been their top priority.

But I didn't blame them. When two people are as deeply in love as Lottie as Asher are, talk is an optional extra.

And then, of course, I'd called them and probably put a bit of a damper on the evening.

Asher chuckled. 'Basically, it's because everyone likes a party. And we want to have it as soon as possible as it's a good way to let everybody know we're engaged.'

I grinned. 'You could put an announcement in the parish newsletter. Perse would love that. Or you could simply tell Lilith Shoe. Everyone would hear about it in five minutes flat.'

Perse, which is short for Persephone and is pronounced as Percy, is the vicar of St Mary Star of the Sea. I'm not really sure how old she is but I do know she was one of the youngest women to become a Reverend. She's only been in Seahorse Harbour for a few years or so, but it seems like she's been here forever. I would say she's in her late thirties now, but she has one of those faces that doesn't seem to age. She's slightly overweight with short, spiky, brilliant-white-blonde hair, and quite large front teeth of the identical colour. She's really lovely, and if it wasn't for her, also brilliant-white, dog collar, you'd never guess she was a vicar.

Lottie and Asher both laughed.

'I suspect Lilith already knows,' Asher said. 'That woman has a knack of knowing everything, almost before it's happened.'

That was a slight exaggeration. But not too far from the truth.

'Then the sooner we get this party organised, the better. What about Friday night? The church hall's not a bad place for it. It's in the centre of the village, everyone knows how to get there, and it'll accommodate everybody, with room to spare.'

'That's not a bad idea.' Asher looked as though I'd made some astonishing revelation as he smiled at Lottie. 'Unless you'd prefer somewhere more glamorous?'

Lottie shook her head, her eyes wide with excitement. 'I think the church hall is perfect. If we can get it. The Meet and Mingle Jingle at Christmas went off really well and the hall looked wonderfully festive. We could decorate it with bunting and balloons, or something. I'm sure it would look beautiful in no time.'

'I'll phone Perse right away and ask her if it's free on Friday.' Asher sounded thrilled. 'I'm really glad you came, Sorcha. Now all you've got to do is sort out the invitations, food for a buffet or whatever, and either a DJ or some other form of music. Can we leave that with you?' He winked at me and laughed.

'We can't expect Sorcha to do everything,

darling.' There was a hint of reprimand in Lottie's tone even though she was smiling. 'And besides, I would like to be involved in arranging our engagement party. It's the only engagement party I'll ever be having.'

'Of course, sweetheart. I was just teasing my sister. I want to be involved in it too. I don't intend to ever have another one either.'

'We'll all do it together,' I said, raising my glass in a toast. Asher and Lottie also raised theirs. 'This will be the best engagement party Seahorse Harbour has ever seen. Here's to you and Lottie. Cheers!'

'Cheers! I love you Asher, and I'm the luckiest girl on the planet.' There was a look of euphoria on Lottie's face even though her voice was tinged with a hint of sadness. 'I still can't believe this is happening. I wish Mum and Dad could've lived to see it. But this has been the best February ever. What with Valentine's Day last weekend and all the amazing presents you gave me. And then on Thursday you made my thirty-fourth birthday a day I'll never forget. And now I'm engaged! And to the most wonderful man in the world.'

Luckily for me, in spite of this being one of the worst Februarys I could recall, having spent the entire week between Valentine's Day and now, wrapped up in my own problems with Sean, I had remembered Lottie's birthday. But only because Asher called and texted several times to remind me.

'And I'm engaged to the most wonderful woman in the Universe.' Asher's expression said it all.

Three

I soon discovered that organising an engagement party in less than a week isn't as easy as I'd thought, even with Lottie and Asher's help. And they weren't the only ones involved. Elsie, Josie and Diana offered their assistance as soon as they heard the news of the engagement. Even Perse, the vicar of St Mary Star of the Sea, got on board.

Luckily, the church hall was available on Friday. Perse didn't charge a fee; she just asked Asher and Lottie to make a small donation to the repair fund for the church.

St Mary Star of the Sea has stood in the centre of Seahorse Harbour since 1069 and although it may be small, the costs of repairs are apparently anything but.

It probably doesn't help that the church sits on high ground and is constantly battered by the salt air. There's a massive, ancient oak tree right beside it which offers some protection from the storms that rush in across the English Channel, but other than that the church is fairly exposed.

The bright yellow bench beneath the ancient oak offers a glorious vista of the bay. A splendid hotel once sat opposite the church. It was built in the mid-1800s, was three storeys high and ran the full length of the road down to the promenade. That would have provided ample shelter, but it was bombed in the Second World War and razed to the ground. A garden of remembrance was erected in its place called Memorial Gardens, where steps lead down to lawned areas and a path meanders towards the beach, surrounded by bushes, plants and an abundance of flowers. So now, other than the partial protection from the ancient oak, the church is open to the elements.

A pretty lychgate leads to the main entrance door to the church, and the hall can be accessed via a door inside the nave. It's fairly well hidden behind a heavy, red velvet curtain and it creaks when it's opened, despite the fact the hinges are oiled regularly by Perse, so Asher told me. There's also a separate entrance to the hall from outside.

The hall itself is a small, wooden building attached to the other side of the church, farthest away from the sea, which means the entrance is fairly sheltered in stormy weather. At this time of year that's handy because there's a lot of stormy weather in Seahorse Harbour in the winter.

Mind you, I've seen some tremendous storms during the summer, especially over the last few years. I don't know if that has anything to do with global warming or not, but storms do seem to be more frequent these days.

Thankfully, the weather so far during the week had been calm and exceptionally mild for the time of year. We were all hoping that it would remain that way on Friday. We'd arranged for bunting, banners, and balloons to be strung all around the outside of the hall, but anything more than a mild breeze would definitely ruin the effect.

More bunting, banners and balloons were hung inside and it didn't take long to transform the shabby chic hall into a virtual, party palace.

Okay, that might be a slight exaggeration, but it did look rather snazzy by the time we'd finished.

Asher and Liam came to help hang all the decorations, but as Alex was still recovering from his near fatal brush with death at Christmas, Diana insisted that the only way she would allow Alex up and down a ladder was over her dead body.

'That's a tempting proposition,' Josie quipped, which resulted in Diana thumping her playfully on her arm.

Unfortunately for me, Asher roped in Nathan Bromley to help. I'd managed to avoid the guy all week, sometimes going to great lengths to do so because frankly I couldn't face either his sarcasm or a patronising comment. Or even worse, insincere sympathy.

When he strolled into the hall, via the church, just after lunchtime on Friday, I can honestly say I felt as if a cloud had descended. I suppose I might have imagined it but it seemed to me that Nathan made a beeline for me within seconds of arriving.

'Hi,' he said, his easy smile reaching his eyes, and his tone fairly enthusiastic, almost as if the man was pleased to see me. 'I heard about your latest break-up. I'm sorry, Sorcha. Are you okay?'

Pleased to be able to have a dig at me, it seemed.

'I'll live. No thanks to you.'

'Me?' The surprise on his face was genuine. 'Where do I fit into it?'

I tutted. 'Don't act all innocent with me. You know full well. But I don't want to talk about it, so you can forget it. If you're here to help, there's a load of trestle tables in that little room over there. You can get those and put them up in straight lines along those two walls.'

I pointed at one of the two small rooms at the end of the hall and then the two walls in front of which we had decided the rows of tables should sit.

He furrowed his brows. 'I really don't

understand.'

'It's pretty simple, Nathan. Trestle tables from that room. Pull out the folding legs. Stand them up in neat, straight lines. Surely even you can manage that without causing too much trouble?'

He puffed out a quick sigh. 'I understand about the tables, Sorcha. What I don't understand is why you seem to feel that I'm in some way to blame for your latest break-up.'

I couldn't help myself. I slapped my notebook against his arm and growled at him. I might have even bared my teeth. Which was probably not a pretty sight. Although I had brushed them after lunch and my breath was minty fresh from several swigs of mouthwash.

'Will you please stop saying "latest"! It's really annoying.'

His frown deepened as he rubbed his arm.

'Sorry. I wasn't doing it intentionally. I was just stating a fact.'

'Facts aren't always helpful. Or correct.'

'Er. Surely the very definition of a fact is that it is correct?'

'No. Sometimes facts are false. Fake facts. Like fake news.'

'Really? You're serious? Hmm. I think we'll have to agree to disagree on that one.'

'Excellent. At least we agree on something. Are you going to deal with the tables? Or do I need to get someone else to do that? We're on a tight time schedule here, you know.'

He held up both hands in a gesture of surrender.

'Okay. I'm on it. But this conversation isn't over. I'm happy to take the blame when I've done something. But I really don't see how I had anything to do with your latest ... I mean, with your recent break-up.'

'Oh, bugger off, Nathan. Can't you see I'm busy?'

I marched off, and I have to tell you, I was fighting a serious urge to batter him with my notebook several times over. The man is just so bloody irritating. No wonder he doesn't have a girlfriend.

Four

Perhaps, bearing in mind the way my life had been going recently, what happened next was inevitable.

I thought it was Destiny. With a capital D ... For 'Delightful'.

Not everyone agreed.

I'm pretty certain Nathan Bromley didn't.

But I didn't care what he thought.

All afternoon I'd had a sort of tingling sensation in my tummy. Almost as if I expected something to happen. Whether it was something good or something bad, I wasn't sure.

At first I thought it was caused by the ham, cheese and pickled onion sandwich I'd eaten for lunch. Followed by a banana muffin. But I'd felt fine when I cleaned my teeth. The tingling only started as I was wondering whether the red dress I had planned to wear to the party was really my best choice.

I had been watching Nathan as he

assembled the tables with ease, and although he set them out in a perfectly straight line, I couldn't help but find fault.

'That one's slightly wonky looking.' I pointed to the offending table.

Without a word he sighed, shook his head, grabbed my notebook and tore out a page which, after handing me back my notebook, he folded several times before bending down and sticking the paper prop under the wobbly leg.

'Now it's not.'

He annoyed me even more by winking and smiling at me.

'I had written something on that page!'

I glowered at him and pursed my lips, which only seemed to increase his smile.

'Yes, I saw it. It said, "Red dress or blue?" and there were two columns. I assume you were about to write a list of pros and cons for each. I can save you some time. Wear the blue. Blue brings out the colour of your eyes.'

I was tempted to hit him with my notebook again but instead I forced a smile.

'Thank you, Nathan. Red it is then.'

I heard him chuckle as I walked away, but the tingling started shortly after and I began to doubt the wisdom of my choice.

I didn't have a great deal of time to think about it. The tables had to be dressed, plates and napkins set out, food and beverages displayed, and at least a hundred other things still needed to be done. Including making space for the dance area and for the DJ.

We'd gone with a DJ, as it was someone from Easterhill who was recommended by Jonno, a villager and a good friend of Asher's. Jonno is also a minicab driver and a handyman, so he's a very useful friend to have. In addition to that he and his wife Sandra are really lovely people.

But there was one little problem. The DJ, who goes by the name of Tiny Blazer (apparently his name's Tim Blazer and he's over six-feet-seven inches tall, so everyone calls him Tiny) was supposed to be with his friends on a bachelor weekend. Luckily, it was taking place in Seahorse Harbour. Jonno said that Tiny was happy to do the gig if his mates could come along to the engagement party.

Well, what could possibly go wrong with that?

Just as we were putting the final touches to the hall, Tiny arrived. Along with six friends, each of whom looked as if they could rugby-tackle for England, and all of whom, apart from Tiny, and possibly one other, must have started consuming alcohol at breakfast. They were definitely having trouble staying upright.

I know what you're thinking. Tiny's friends would wreck the place.

Nope. That's not what happened at all.

What happened was, I fell in love.

I didn't mean to. Really I didn't. This was Asher and Lottie's night and I had planned to devote my time and attention to ensuring it went off without a hitch. But the minute the other sober friend turned and stared directly at me, I could feel my jaw drop, my eyes pop out of my head, my heart do a somersault, and my brain explode.

He was blond, broad-shouldered, big – as in tall – and utterly beautiful. Yes. Beautiful. He had the face of an angel and eyes to match. His smile was like a ray of sunshine inside the hall. I wouldn't have been at all surprised if a halo hung over his head. There did seem to be a glow behind him, but I later realised that was from the set of disco lights Tiny had started testing.

It was a magical moment. The Adonis and I stood staring at one another and although I could hear Nathan's voice close by, I didn't hear a word he said.

The vision slowly walked towards me, that gorgeous smile getting brighter with each step and when he stopped, just inches from me and looked down into my eyes, I'm pretty sure I gasped.

At that moment, I did hear Nathan sigh and groan, 'Oh dear God. Not again.'

'Hello,' the god-like man said, his voice like a soft caress. 'I'm Finlay Demon. And I think you're the most beautiful woman I've ever seen.'

Don't judge me. I know that sounds like a line but if you'd heard the way he said it and seen the look on that glorious face and the sparkle in those incredible, blue eyes, you'd have been bowled over too.

My mouth moved up and down but no words came out for at least five seconds.

'Demon? As in devil?'

Okay. That was a stupid thing to say.

He grinned at me.

'Demon by name but not by nature.'

'Oh.' I sounded almost disappointed, even to my ears. 'That's good. I've had enough bad boys to last a lifetime.'

He raised one brow and I shook my head.

'No,' I added. 'That didn't come out right. What I meant was that I don't have much luck with men. I seem to pick the bad ones.'

'Not anymore,' he said, almost whispering in my ear as he leaned towards me.

Asher broke the spell.

'Excuse me for interrupting,' he said, taking my arm in an unusually firm hold. 'Lottie's asking if you'd go home with her and help her get ready. Apparently, you promised you would make her look stunning, and, although I think she always looks breathtaking, she's fairly adamant that she needs you. Right now.'

He gave Finlay an apologetic smile but it

wasn't as warm as Asher's smiles usually were.

'Oh. Er. Yes, I did say that.' I didn't want to leave.

Finlay reached out and briefly took my fingers in his.

'I'll be here. Right here, when you come back. But at least tell me your name before you go.'

'Sorcha. My name's Sorcha. I'll be back as soon as I can.'

'And I'm Asher. Her older brother.' Asher stepped between us. 'And I'm not going anywhere.'

Finlay smiled. 'Pleased to meet you, Asher. Thank you for letting us crash your party. You have my word we'll behave. And that your sister will be safe with me.'

'Hmm.' Asher didn't sound convinced. 'I hope so. I would hate for anything to spoil this engagement party. Anything at all. Come along, Sorcha. Please don't keep Lottie waiting. This is her special night, don't forget.'

I felt as if I'd been told off as Asher led me away but when I glanced over my shoulder, I saw Finlay Demon smiling at me, and he was positively glowing. Or perhaps it was the disco lights again.

I also glimpsed Nathan Bromley standing near to Finlay – and he definitely wasn't glowing.

In fact, I think Nathan was scowling.

He really is a miserable, judgemental git.

Five

I think every single person in Seahorse Harbour attended Lottie and Asher's engagement party.

Mum and Dad had driven down that morning. Normally they would have stayed at Asher's, along with me, but now that Lottie and her dog, Merry were as good as living there, they decided his cottage might be a bit cramped, and instead they booked a room at Lilith Shoe's, Sunrise B&B.

Lottie was a bit upset by this. She had only met Mum and Dad once, when the three of us popped down for a day in January, specifically to meet her, and although she had been terrified by the prospect of meeting Asher's family, she believed we all liked her. Which we did. Now Mum and Dad were staying elsewhere, she wasn't quite so sure, and it took Asher and me a while to convince her that they were doing it because they *did* like her, not because they didn't.

'They don't want to be in our way,' he told her.

'Why would they feel they were in our way?' she responded.

'Because the cottage is a little small for five people and a dog.'

'Then Merry and I should be the ones to stay elsewhere. I can go and stay at Mum's.'

'No. I want you here with me. You and Merry.'

'But your parents always stay with you. Along with Sorcha.'

'Yes. And it's always very cramped with just the four of us.'

'Look,' I said. 'I love Mum and Dad to bits, but I'm rather glad they're not staying here. Mum has a tendency to get up in the night and wander around, half naked. Believe me, Lottie, that's a sight you really don't want to see. She says it's due to hot flushes and the menopause. And Dad snores so loudly the walls virtually rattle. They're doing you and Asher a favour. They probably think you might change your mind about marrying him if you see the family you're getting yourself into. Honestly, Lottie. They really like you. In years to come, you'll be wishing they would stay somewhere else.'

I'm not sure Lottie was totally convinced even though I was telling her the truth.

'But I want to be part of your family,' she said. 'And I want your parents to feel as comfortable around me as possible.'

Asher wrapped his arms around her. 'And they want the same. We all do. Just not this weekend, okay?'

She hesitated as if she wanted to debate the matter further but eventually she gave a small smile and said, 'Okay.'

But I got the feeling that Mum and Dad staying elsewhere had taken a bit of the shine off of Lottie's engagement weekend.

She perked up later, especially as Mum and Dad made a concerted effort to shower her with attention and affection. I think they managed to put to rest any lingering doubts she had regarding how they felt about her.

I was pleased to see Asher's good friend from Easterhill, Terry Ford and Terry's fiancée, Sarah, along with Terry's sister Molly and her fiancé, Chance. I wasn't surprised by Terry and Sarah's engagement at Christmas, but I was astonished to hear about Molly and Chance, just after New Year. We weren't sure if they would make it to the party because Chance's mum, Vicky had breast cancer surgery in January and it was touch and go for a while. Thankfully though, she pulled through, and is now recovering well. The prognosis is good, and Vicky is looking forward to a bright future with Bruce, the new man in her life.

It seems as if everyone is either getting engaged, or is in a serious relationship, apart from me.

Diana, Alex and their teenaged-children, Becca and Toby, together with Noah, Becca's lovely boyfriend were huddled near the door with Josie and Liam, and Liam's daughter Orla, along with her boyfriend, Darren. They were chatting with Elsie and when Asher, Lottie and I arrived, Lottie and Asher headed towards them.

The first thing I did, was scan the room for Finlay Demon.

To my amazement, he was exactly where he said he would be; at the very spot at which I'd left him.

He smiled at me and his admiring glances as he looked me up and down sent shivers racing through me and I had difficulty walking towards him. I actually wanted to run but that would've been a bit undignified. Not that dignity was something I often worried about, but this was Lottie and Asher's night and the last thing I wanted to do was draw attention to me.

I took a deep breath and returned Finlay's gorgeous smile.

'Please don't tell me you've been standing here all this time?'

'I said I'd be here, and I am.'

I tilted my head to one side and grinned at him.

'But you've moved, haven't you?'

He laughed, and the sound made the shivers double in intensity.

'I could say no, but that wouldn't be true. I've moved several times, mainly because I am supposed to be at a bachelor party with my mates, not standing around waiting for a beautiful stranger to come back to me. And once because I needed the loo. That's not quite as romantic, I know, but it is the truth.'

'Truth is good. I like the truth.'

'Then I'll tell you another truth. You look absolutely sensational. Blue brings out the colour in your eyes.'

I wished he hadn't said that, in a way. It reminded me of what Nathan had said earlier, and the fact that Nathan's comment might have made me change my decision on what I was going to wear, irritated me. Even if I'd done so not for Nathan's benefit but to increase my chances with Finlay.

'That wasn't a line,' Finlay added. 'Blue really suits you.'

He must've seen the expression on my face as I had remembered Nathan's words, and assumed I doubted his sincerity.

'Thanks. I wasn't sure about this dress but now I'm glad I chose it.'

'So am I.' He held out his hand and I placed mine in his without hesitation. 'Dancing isn't my speciality but if you're willing to take a chance with me I'll try not to tread on your toes.

I think Tiny's playing our song.'

I was more than willing, and when I realised the song Tiny was playing was a George Michael classic, wild horses wouldn't have stopped me.

I've got a bit of a thing for George Michael's music, thanks to Mum listening to it when I was growing up, and this one with Aretha Franklin did seem to be rather appropriate. It's called *I Knew You Were Waiting (For Me)* and I did wonder if Finlay Demon could read my mind or something.

'You couldn't possibly know this,' I said as we took to the dance floor, 'but I love this song.'

His smile sent a whole new batch of sensations running around my body and when he pulled me into his arms and gently spun me around, and out and back again, I was fairly certain my luck with men had finally changed. We weren't doing a particular dance or anything. Just moving together in time to the music but it felt as if I was floating above the room.

'I'd like to say I knew, but that wouldn't be true. I overheard your brother ask Tiny earlier if he would play it this evening. When I heard the title, I thought it was apt, so I admit I asked Tiny to play it soon after I gave him a signal. Which I did the moment I saw you come back.'

I smiled as I looked up into his eyes.

'Are you for real? Do you usually go to such

lengths when you see a woman you like?'

'No. But who says I like you?'

There was laughter in his eyes which was suddenly replaced with a serious intensity and he pulled me up against him. The sensations I felt right then almost knocked me off my feet and his next sentence made my heart soar.

'Do you believe in love at first sight, Sorcha?'

Six

How I managed to remain standing, I have no idea. Or what stopped me from ripping the man's clothes off and making insanely passionate love to him on the spot.

All the previous heartache and pain was worth it to bring me to this moment. This wonderful, unbelievable moment when I was standing in front of this incredibly handsome man who was telling me he had fallen in love with me at first sight.

It was as if all the stars had aligned just for this.

Okay, I know that might sound sickeningly gushy, and also somewhat clichéd, but that's how it felt, I promise you.

Nothing could ruin this. Not even the glimpse I got of Nathan Bromley's face as he passed by us, with his aunt Lyn, who tapped me on the arm.

'Hello, Sorcha,' she said. 'Isn't this a wonderful party? I heard you were back this week and helped organise it but I haven't seen you in the café. I'm so glad to see that beautiful smile back on your face, and you look so pretty this evening. But who is this young man? I don't know you, do I?'

'Oh hi, Lyn. Yeah. I've been a bit busy. I've been meaning to pop in and say hello but you know how it is. Time flies. This is Finlay. He's here on holiday.'

I don't know why I said that but Finlay held out his hand and smiled at her.

'It's really just a long weekend for my mate's bachelor party. It's lovely to meet you, Lyn. You're looking very pretty yourself.'

Lyn tapped him on the arm and giggled like a schoolgirl.

'Oh get away with you. It's been a decade or two since I looked pretty, but thank you for the thought. This is Nathan, my nephew. He's a godsend. He's helping me out at my café on the promenade. We serve a really good breakfast and we're open early on a Sunday.' She winked at Finlay as she linked her arm through Nathan's and edged him forward.

Nathan gave Finlay a brief smile and they sort of nodded at one another.

'I see you went with the blue dress, after all,' Nathan said, with something between a sneer and a smile on his lips.

I couldn't think of anything witty or sarcastic to say, so I simply threw him a similar sneering smile.

'Are you and Sorcha *friends*?' Lyn asked, putting an odd emphasis on the word 'friends' and glancing down at our interlocked hands.

Finlay let go of my hand and wrapped his arm around my waist and the gesture made my heart do a little dance.

'Yes, we are. And hopefully, so much more,' he said.

All three of us stared at him but his smile was genuine and he looked totally sincere. I felt as if I'd won the lottery, while Nathan looked as if he'd lost the shirt off his back, and Lyn – well, Lyn looked as if she didn't believe a word of it.

She tapped my arm again. 'Have fun, sweetheart, but remember the old saying, 'Don't rush in'.'

She didn't finish it. She didn't have to. We all knew what she meant and frankly, I was a bit peeved, but Ed Sheeran's song, *Perfect* started playing and Nathan gave me a cursory nod and led her away, gently holding her in his arms like the caring nephew he clearly was.

'Sorry about that,' I said, glancing up into Finlay's dreamy eyes and hoping to recapture the magic. 'She had no right to say that.'

'There's nothing to be sorry about.' His smile was reassuring. 'She obviously cares about you, and that's a good thing. Plus, it's wise advice. Sadly, it's too late for me.' He held me close again. 'I'm already in too deep.'

The magic was back and I felt wonderful.

I still couldn't quite believe this was happening, but from the moment I had first seen Finlay, earlier in the day, it was as if I knew him. As if I'd known him for years and years. It felt so right. It felt so good.

And in spite of Finlay's friends trying to entice him away from me with promises of copious amounts of alcohol and some rather crazy sounding dares, and Asher's attempts to prize us apart on more than one occasion, Finlay and I managed to spend most of the party together.

I can honestly say I couldn't remember the last time I'd had such a lovely evening and I didn't want it to end. But like all good things, I knew it would.

Except it didn't. Finlay made sure of that.

'Want to sneak out of here before my mates – and your very protective brother come and find us?'

I didn't even hesitate.

'Absolutely. Where to?'

He took a second to think.

'We're all staying at the Seahorse Harbour Holiday Park, in a couple of the caravans, so I can't take you to mine. What about yours?'

I shook my head. 'I'm staying at my brother's cottage, so that's out.'

'It's too cold to be outside for long.' He scanned the room as if a solution might be lurking somewhere. 'What about the nightclub I saw on the promenade this afternoon? It's not exactly private but nightclubs always have dark corners, and I really want to kiss you right now, away from prying eyes.'

I'm sure I made a shriek of delight because all I'd been thinking about for the last hour or so was what it would feel like to kiss and be kissed by Finlay Demon.

'Neptune's!' I said. 'Yes. Although the owner is a friend of my brother. But he isn't always there, and he's here at the moment because I saw him loitering near Diana. They had an affair and … oh God. Why am I babbling about them? Sorry. I think I'm over excited or something.'

'I'm feeling the same. I could be sixteen again and about to share my first kiss, the way my heart is beating. Does being in love always feel like this? I haven't been in love for a while, so I can't remember.'

He took my hand and placed it on his chest and while I couldn't exactly say I could feel his heart pounding, mine definitely was. His chest was firm and muscular in all the right places and I could feel the warmth of his skin through his shirt. Not in a sweaty, gross way but in a sexy, welcoming one. I couldn't wait to touch that skin and feel his flesh beneath my hands. But we couldn't do that in Neptune's nightclub.

'Finlay?'

'Yes?'

'I ... I don't want you to get the wrong impression of me, because this isn't something I usually do – or say – but how would you feel if I suggested we get a room somewhere?'

He sucked in a breath and his hold on me tightened. He leaned even closer and whispered in my ear.

'I'd say you've just made my dreams come true. Do you have somewhere in mind?'

My breath was coming in gasps and I couldn't believe what I'd suggested. I usually wait for the man to make the first move, but with Finlay, I didn't want to wait.

'There's only the Holiday Park and the Sunrise B&B in the village, but my parents are staying at the B&B and your friends are staying at the Holiday Park, so that might be awkward. The only other place I can think of right now is the Easterhill Hotel. But that's in Easterhill, obviously, which is about four miles from here.'

'We can get a cab. Four miles isn't far. Although it feels like the distance to the moon at the moment. I can't believe how badly I want you. Shall I call and see if they have a room?'

I was about to say, 'Yes P-L-E-A-S-E!' But from the corner of my eye, I saw Diana running and tears were streaming down her face. Diana was a bit like me in that she didn't run. Ever. As far as I knew. And I'd only seen her cry, once, so this was something serious. As much as I wanted to disappear with Finlay, I somehow felt obliged to see why she was so upset. No one else seemed to have noticed but as I quickly searched the room for Alex and saw him surrounded by Finlay's friends, I had a feeling of dread.

'Finlay! What are your friends doing to Alex?'

I grabbed his hand and darted towards the group, almost dragging Finlay with me. They were all in one corner of the hall and unbelievably, everyone else appeared to be having so much fun they hadn't noticed the unfolding scene.

Thankfully, it wasn't what I thought. Finlay's friends were laughing and teasing Alex and patting him on the back. I didn't understand why that would upset Diana, but I needed to find out before I went after her.

'What's going on?' Finlay asked before I had the chance.

'Hey mate!' One of the drunken men pulled Finlay into a bear hug but he quickly released himself. 'You'll never guess who this guy is. You won't, so I'll tell you. It's Alex Dunn.'

Finlay furrowed his brows. 'Alex Dunn? The name does sound vaguely familiar but I don't think I know him. Who's Alex Dunn?'

'This guy,' the drunk friend said, slapping a pale and sheepish looking Alex on the back.

'What I meant was, why is he important,

and, more to the point, why does the poor guy look uncomfortable with your attention, Andy?'

'Probably because he shagged my wife,' Andy said, grinning from ear to ear.

'Ah,' Finlay said, darting a quick look at me. 'I see. Yes. Now I remember.' He gave me a relieved smile. 'There's no need to worry. Andy is just showing his appreciation. His wife wasn't great and she treated Andy appallingly. Finding out about her affair with Alex here, actually did Andy a favour. Although it did take him a while to feel that way.'

'Bloody hell! Well, that's a surprise, although it shouldn't be. The point is, Alex nearly died just a couple of months ago so this isn't helping his recovery. Can you get your friends to back off, please?'

'Jesus! Of course.'

Finlay edged his way closer to Alex and freed him from the clutches of Andy and the rest of the group who had all been vigorously patting Alex on the back. Alex was clearly relieved.

'Thanks. I wasn't sure how drunk they were and sometimes it's best to remain passive, rather than behave aggressively. Did you see where Diana went?'

He glanced around, smoothing his clothes back into place. His shirt had been pulled out and his sweater was hanging from one shoulder. Alex liked to be pristine, so I think being manhandled and dishevelled was more upsetting to him than anything else. He certainly wasn't a weak or cowardly man, but his brush with death had changed him, in more ways than one, perhaps.

'Yes. She went that way,' I said, pointing towards the entrance to the church. 'She was crying, Alex. Did these men hurt her?'

'My mates wouldn't hurt a woman.' Finlay jumped to his friends' defence but his voice was reassuring, not argumentative.

Alex shook his head. 'No.' He seemed unsure whether to continue but he added, 'I promised I'd told her about all of my affairs, but it seems I hadn't.' He leaned forward so that only Finlay and I could hear, the group now all forming some sort of rugby scrum amongst themselves. 'I'd completely forgotten about … er…'

'Veronica,' Finlay offered.

'Veronica. Yes. I'm afraid she slipped my mind.'

I noticed Finlay's jaw clench, as if Alex had annoyed him.

'Alex!' I snapped. 'I'd heard you've had several affairs, but really? You've had so many you can't even remember all their names? No wonder Diana's upset.'

'But that's all in the past. I've changed. Diana knows that. I'd better go and find her.

Excuse me.'

Finlay and I stepped aside as Andy turned towards us.

'Hey! Where did the guy go? I wanted to buy him a drink.'

'Don't waste your money,' Finlay said. He glanced at me. 'The guy may be a friend of yours but he's a total shit if he forgets the name of the women he's slept with. Does breaking up another person's marriage mean so little to him? Sorry. I shouldn't take that out on you.'

'You haven't. And I agree. He's not really a friend. Diana is. I suppose he is a friend of Asher's but not a close one. Although actually, I'm not sure Asher likes him much. There's nothing to apologise for. But it really is a small world. How did Veronica and Alex meet? I know Tiny's local, but where are the rest of you from?'

'London. Tiny's from London too. He inherited a cottage in Easterhill from his gran when she died a few years ago, and now he spends his time between his flat in London and the cottage, which isn't big enough to swing a cat. Although why anyone would want to swing a cat is beyond me. As for Veronica, she met Alex when he performed heart surgery on her dad. I don't know the details, only that they began their affair shortly after and it lasted for several months. I think Veronica was pretty serious about the guy but he clearly didn't feel the same.'

'Come on mate,' Andy tugged at Finlay's arm. 'It's supposed to be my bachelor party and you've spent all night with this lovely woman. I don't blame you, 'cos she's gorgeous, but mates are mates and now it's time you came with us.'

Finlay looked torn as he tried to prize his arm free but all the others had joined in so it took him a while.

'Okay, okay! Just give me a minute will you, guys?'

They released him and he turned back to me, shaking his head.

'I don't know what to do. I want to be with you, you know that, don't you? But they're right. I did come here for Andy's bachelor weekend and I haven't spent more than five minutes with him. Would you hate me if I abandoned you and went with them now? From the look of it, I think they might need my help to get back to the Holiday Park, although Tiny's relatively sober, I assume. And I'm not really abandoning you because I want to see you again as soon as possible. Tomorrow? Can I see you? Please? We're here till Tuesday morning, so although I will need to spend time with them over the next few days, I can also be with you. If you want to be with me, that is. Do you want to be with me, Sorcha?'

'Do you really need to ask? I thought I'd made that pretty clear. And don't worry about abandoning me. You're right. You probably should be with your friends. Plus, I should help clear this place up later, so I need to stay, even though I'd rather run off with you.'

I laughed but in reality I was utterly disappointed. If only I hadn't seen Diana. Finlay and I might've been spending the night in each other's arms. Instead, he'd be taking care of his drunken mates, and I'd be cleaning tables and loading the dishwasher.

'We can run off together tomorrow. But I'll be thinking about you all night.'

The look in his eyes made my insides turn to mush and I wished there was some way we could spend the night together. But the anticipation would only make it better when we did.

'And I'll be thinking about you. Is it really Andy's bachelor party? When did his marriage to Veronica break-up?'

'About eight years ago, but he kept going back to her. It was only when he met his current fiancée, Suzie, that he realised the insanity of that, and finally told Veronica it was over. That was three years ago.'

'And he knew it was Alex his wife had an affair with? I'm amazed he could remember Alex's name. Especially in his present inebriated state.'

Finlay frowned. 'I don't think Andy will ever completely forget about Alex Dunn. I had,

I admit. But Andy was crazy about Veronica and her betrayal nearly broke him. It's only the last three years that have made him realise how toxic the woman was and how lucky he is to now have Suzie. But even so, I'm surprised he behaved the way he did just now. I don't think I would've blamed him if he'd punched Alex in the face. All the alcohol he's consumed must've mellowed him.'

'It's a good thing he didn't. Especially taking into account Alex's current condition.'

'That's true.'

'Would you have hit Alex if you'd been Andy?'

I don't know why I asked that but I was glad Finlay seemed to consider it.

'No. I don't think so. But none of us knows how we will act in a situation until we experience it for ourselves.'

'Are you coming, mate?' Andy called out, clearly having trouble staying upright now, one arm leant against the wall.

'Be right there.' Finlay smiled at me. 'I'd better go. I really want to kiss you but I don't want everyone to watch.'

'I want to kiss you too, but Mum and Dad and my brother might not approve, and while I don't really care what they might think right now, this is my brother's engagement party and people should be concentrating on him and Lottie, not talking about me kissing a total stranger. Except you don't feel like a stranger. I feel as if I've known you all my life.'

'Same here,' he said. 'I'll see you tomorrow and we can pick up where we left off.' He squeezed my fingers as he turned to go. 'Oh shit!' He quickly turned back to me. 'I need your phone number or I won't be able to call you in the morning.'

'Good thinking! Although at least I know where you're staying. And everyone in the village knows who I am.'

That didn't sound quite the way I intended, but I sent him my phone number via a text, with an emoji heart and he smiled when it pinged and he saw it. He sent a heart emoji back.

'Until tomorrow then, Sorcha. Get home safely tonight. And make sure you dream of me.'

He winked and smiled and turned to his friends, but as I watched him walk away into the throng of people towards Tiny who was starting to pack up his equipment, I saw him turn and glance back at me at least twice. And before his group finally left the hall, I noticed him looking at me more than once. A couple of times he even waved and I thought he might change his mind and decide to leave his friends to their own devices, but he didn't.

In a strange way, I was glad of that. It meant he wasn't the sort of man who would totally abandon his friends when something more exciting came along. And didn't that indicate that he was a fundamentally decent man? The complete opposite of most of the previous men I'd dated.

Yep. My luck had definitely changed.

I'd met Finlay Demon and I was pretty sure he could be The One.

Seven

'I feel sorry for Diana,' Lottie said, as we discussed the events of the previous night over a full blown English breakfast.

'So do I,' I said. 'But she knew what she was letting herself in for when she took Alex back. Although he maintains all that's behind him. And this other affair was several years ago, so I'm not sure why she was quite so upset.'

'Probably just shock,' Asher said. 'She thought she knew everything about his past after he came clean, so maybe she is wondering if there's anything else she doesn't know.'

I shrugged. 'Perhaps. But it was a bit dramatic to run off like that.'

Asher sort of sneered. 'Diana's always been a little dramatic, at least she has since I've known her. I like her, of course, but let's not forget she didn't treat Mikkel very well, did she?'

'No, she bloody didn't.' That was true, and frankly, I believed Mikkel deserved better.

‘We reap what we sow,’ Lottie said. ‘That’s what my mum always used to say. My other mum.’ She gave a little grin. ‘I hope Diana and Alex work it out though.’

‘They will.’ I helped myself to more coffee from the pot on the table. ‘Let’s face it, Diana adores him and she’ll forgive him anything.’ I saw Asher eyeing me with concern. ‘What?’

He shook his head. ‘Nothing. What about you? Did you have a good time last night?’

‘I did, thanks. I had a brilliant time.’ I beamed at him and grabbed another slice of toast from the plate beside the coffee pot.

Asher passed me the butter dish. He always uses a butter dish. He hates seeing a plastic carton of butter on the table, or worse still, a tattered wrapper with butter oozing out of the sides. I did that once and he went on about it for a week. Well, maybe not a week, but it felt like it.

‘You and that guy, Finlay spent a lot of time together.’

I suppose it was inevitable that he would question me about Finlay at some point, and to be honest, I was surprised he hadn’t interrogated me last night. But I suppose he had other things on his mind. Like his fiancée. The pair of them spent most of the party wrapped up in one another, so I’m actually surprised he noticed me and Finlay. But then again, Asher has always watched out for me, and I suppose old habits die hard. It was probably just as well that I hadn't gone to the Easterhill Hotel with Finlay. Asher might've sent out a search party.

After Finlay and his friends left, Mum and Dad, Elsie, Josie and Liam, along with Perse and various others, stayed on to help clear up. Lottie and Asher did too, but we all told them they should let us do it, and they should continue to enjoy their special night. We didn't have to tell them twice. Asher asked me if I would do him a huge favour, and take Merry out for a quick pee before I went to bed, and of course I agreed. After that I didn't see them for dust, until breakfast.

Unfortunately for me, I did see Nathan Bromley.

'Hi, Sorcha,' he said, suddenly appearing from nowhere and giving me the shock of my life.

'Dear God, Nathan! You almost gave me a heart attack. What are you doing here?'

I had taken Merry down to the beach, which was merely a stone's throw from Asher's cottage in Rope Way. It must've been well past midnight and although several cottages still had their lights on, the streets were deserted, most of the partygoers having left the church hall at least fifteen to thirty minutes earlier. It was one of those cold, crisp nights and the ebony sky was clear save for myriad stars.

There aren't that many streetlights in Seahorse Harbour, but with the lights from the cottages and the three quarters full moon, which seemed even brighter than usual last night, I didn't need the torch on my phone to see my way.

I was standing on the promenade, marvelling at the majesty of the night sky and if I'm honest, thinking about what I could've been doing other than waiting around in the freezing cold for Lottie's dog to pee, when Nathan startled me.

'Sorry. I thought you'd seen me locking up.'

'Locking up?' I glanced past him towards Seahorse Bites Café. 'Oh. The café.' I frowned at him. 'Did you forget to do it earlier then?'

'Of course not.' He sounded slightly offended by such a suggestion. 'I popped down after seeing Lyn home because I wasn't ready for sleep, so I thought I'd get some stuff prepared for the morning.'

He smiled suddenly, and with the moonlight dancing on his sandy-coloured hair and weather-tanned face, he actually wasn't bad-looking. I almost saw what Elsie, Josie and Diana meant.

But he paled in comparison to Finlay Demon, obviously.

'Is there much to prepare at a bijou, beach café?'

The smile vanished, his shoulders went

back and his chest puffed out as if he were about to go into battle.

'You'd be surprised.'

'Sorry. I didn't mean that quite the way you obviously think I did. It was a serious question. What do you need to prepare?'

'The ovens and grills all need to be spotless and working. The tables, chairs and floors need cleaning too, in the café, the kitchen, and the toilets. The fridges, freezers and cupboard stock need checking and replenishing. All the food is prepared fresh each day, but it's all the other things behind the scenes that take the time. And then there's the bookkeeping to be done and bills to be sorted and paid. The café may be small but you know yourself how busy it gets. Frankly, I don't know how Lyn has managed to keep the place going on her own.'

'She's not on her own now. She has you.'

'Temporarily, yes. But I might not be around forever.'

'You won't?' That surprised me. 'I thought that was why you came. I heard you were going to be taking over and giving Lyn time to enjoy her retirement.'

He held my gaze for a moment and I have to say, it was a little unsettling, although I'm not sure why.

'You shouldn't believe everything you hear, Sorcha. For one thing, you know my aunt. Retirement is a dirty word as far as she's concerned. Opening this café with my uncle was her dream – and she still has plans for the place. Things she and he discussed but didn't get around to before he died. For another, I have dreams of my own and they don't involve running a café on the promenade ... although they could if...'

'If what?'

He seemed flustered. As if he'd nearly divulged a state secret or something. He averted his eyes, gave a small cough and shook his head.

'Nothing. I don't think my future lies in Seahorse Harbour.'

'Why not? It's a magical place. I love coming here.'

He brightened a touch. 'But you wouldn't live here, would you?'

'Only because there's nowhere to live. Property here is like gold dust. The minute somewhere comes up for sale or for rent, it's snapped up in a matter of seconds.'

'So ... you'd consider living here? Seriously? If you could.'

'Er. Yes. I think so. But that's never going to happen, is it? I'd need a job, and there aren't any around here. I'd need a place to live, and we've already covered that. And, let's be honest, I'd need a relationship, and there's no one around here I would be interested in.'

His mood darkened. 'Of course. I'd

forgotten you can't seem to survive without a man ... Shit! Sorry. I didn't mean that. That was cruel. Forgive me.'

'Nothing to forgive. You're right. And I'm happy to admit it. Don't look so surprised. I think I probably can survive without a man in my life, but the simple truth is, I don't want to. I want to be in a relationship. I want to be in love and to be loved. I don't like being single. I know that's not the way I'm supposed to feel but I do feel that way. It might scare some men off. It might make me sound pathetic and needy. I don't care. It's who I am and it's what I want. And the right man will love me even more for being honest about it. And this may surprise you, Nathan, but I think, tonight, I've finally found that man.'

'You have?'

His voice sounded croaky and there was an odd look of hope mingled with disbelief and wonderment and excitement, all rolled into one.

'I have. And his name is Finlay Demon.'

He blinked and stared at me like I'd told him he was about to die or something.

'F ... Finlay Demon! The guy you just met tonight? Seriously? For fu...flipping hell. You're unbelievable, Sorcha. You really are. You don't know a thing about him.'

'Don't talk to me like that! I don't know why you're so angry. It's not as if you have any right to be. We may be friends, Nathan, but I've never asked – or wanted – your advice on my love life. And for your information, I do know him. I feel as if I've known him all my life. And Finlay feels the same about me. This is Destiny. We are meant for one another. I know we are. And he feels that too. If it hadn't been for Diana and Alex's little drama tonight, we'd be in bed together right now. Tomorrow we will be. And I don't care what you, or Asher, or anyone else has to say about it. You may not believe in love at first sight but I do. And so does Finlay. He's already said he's fallen in love with me. And this time it's for real. This time it'll last. Finlay Demon is The One. So you can keep your opinions and comments to yourself, thank you very much.'

I tugged at Merry's lead and turned to storm off, but Merry went in the wrong direction and got the extended lead caught around Nathan's legs. I hadn't realised how solidly built the bloody man is, because instead of being tripped up, as you might expect him to be, it was me and Merry who were pulled back towards him. Well, mainly Merry, because she's so much smaller. But the foolish dog went the wrong way again and now the lead was twisted around Nathan's calves, and he couldn't have moved if he'd wanted to. Or maybe he could, but he didn't.

He smiled down at Merry, ruffled her fur

with one hand, and tugged at the lead with the other.

'I know you don't want to be near me,' he said, his voice now totally lacking in emotion, 'but you need to give me some slack on the lead so that I can untangle it.'

'Or you could just walk Merry around your legs to do that.'

'Or you could come here and circle around me. That would have the desired result.'

'I'm not coming near you.'

He raised one brow and sighed. 'Seriously? Then just let go of the lead and let me do it.'

'Merry might run off.'

'She won't run off. I've got her.'

'Oh all right. But hurry up. It's freezing out here and I want to go to bed.'

I let the lead go as a strange smile hovered on Nathan's lips. He was bending down but he shot me an odd look from beneath the thick lock of hair that had fallen across his forehead.

'Is that an offer?'

'What? Don't be bloody ridiculous. You're the last person I'd want to go to bed with. Besides. Are you deaf? I just told you I'm in love with Finlay Demon.'

He untangled Merry and walked her towards me, his hand stretched out holding the lead.

He came a little too close for my liking. I could smell his aftershave. Not that it smelt unpleasant. It was actually rather nice. But the look in his eyes wasn't. It was ... well I'm not sure what it was, but it made me feel uneasy, as if the man had some mischief or something planned that somehow included me.

'I heard you, Sorcha. But you've been in love before. Several times, in fact. And we know how each of those turned out. We may be having a similar conversation in a matter of weeks. Or on Wednesday, after the guy has left.'

I gasped. 'That's really mean.'

He shook his head. 'You're right. It was. I'm sorry. But you make me ... so cross sometimes. You can't see what's right in front of you. I almost want to grab you by the arms and...'

'And what? Grab me by the arms and what, Nathan?'

He sighed loudly and ran a hand through his hair, shaking his head at the same time.

'I don't know, Sorcha.' His eyes darted from me to the distance and back to me again and he sighed once more. 'Grab you by the arms and ... and shake some sense into you.'

'Shake some sense into me? Now you're saying I'm stupid? God, Nathan. You make me cross too. Really cross. And if you ever grab me by the arms – or anything else – and try to shake me or ... or anything, I'll scream to high heaven and I'll kick you somewhere it'll really hurt. Hard. Very hard. So don't even think about it, okay? And we won't be having a similar conversation. Ever. Finlay is The One. I know he is. And even if, by some cruel twist of Fate, he isn't, there's one thing I can assure you, Nathan bloody Bromley. You will never be The One. Not ever. Not even for a one-night hook up, because if I'm ever that desperate for sex, you'd be the last person I'd come to.'

I wasn't certain any of what I'd said made sense but I didn't care. This time I did storm off and he didn't say a word in response.

It was only after I got back to the cottage, tumbled into bed and went over and over our conversation that I realised some of what we'd just said to one another.

I think, but I'm not sure, that Nathan sort of said he might like to go to bed with me, if the opportunity ever arose. And I think I made it clear that I'd never, ever go to bed with him, even if things didn't work out with Finlay. Which they would. So it was all irrelevant anyway.

But even during breakfast, I kept wondering if Nathan had really said what I thought he had. Or was he just making fun of me? He'd definitely called me stupid.

Or had I misunderstood our entire conversation completely?

'Are you seeing him again?' Asher asked, after a lengthy silence as I lashed butter on my toast.

'Nathan? Absolutely not.' I bit hard into my slice of toast.

'Nathan?' Asher and Lottie exchanged glances. 'Who mentioned Nathan? I was talking about that guy, Finlay. And please put the lid back on the butter dish.'

Asher didn't give me a chance. He did it for me. I had my hands full anyway. Toast in one, coffee in the other.

I swallowed the mouthful I'd taken, and coughed.

'Oops. That went down the wrong way. Er. I thought someone said, "Nathan". No? And yes. I'm seeing Finlay again. He's going to call me this morning.'

More looks passed between Lottie and Asher.

'Is he single?' Asher was frowning.

'Yes. He's single.' I gave him my best Cheshire-cat-like grin.

Actually, I hadn't asked. But he was, of course. He had to be. He wouldn't have said the things he had if he wasn't.

'How old is he?'

'Around your age.'

I had no idea. I hadn't asked that either. He looked about mid-thirties, but as Jonno was friends with Tiny, who was Finlay's friend, I assumed they might all be late thirties.

'What does he do?'

'I didn't ask for his CV.'

'Funny. Didn't he say?'

'The subject didn't come up.'

'I saw him at the make-shift bar getting some drinks,' Lottie said, 'and he has lovely hands. Not as lovely as yours, darling.' She darted a loving look at Asher. 'But you know what I mean. The kind of hands men have if they've worked in an office environment all their lives. Or are a vet, or a doctor, or something. Not doing heavy manual work, I mean.'

'Does it matter?' I took another bite of toast.

'Only if he doesn't have a job.' Asher was staring at his hands.

He was probably wondering if they were lovely really, or if Lottie had just said that because she loved him.

'I haven't got a job at the moment. What does that say about me?' I didn't try to hide the sarcasm in my tone.

'It says you don't need to have one right now. Although I wish you would find something that could really make you happy.'

'Er. I don't have a job either.' Lottie sounded a bit concerned. And also a little apologetic.

'Nice one, Ash.' I grinned at him. 'How deep is that hole you've dug?'

He reached out and took Lottie's hand.

'Not through any fault of your own, Angel. And you don't need one either. Unless you want one. I know it shouldn't be, but it's different for men. A man without a job often feels as if he's failed somehow.'

'Women feel that too.' Lottie smiled wanly.

'Keep digging, Ash.' I munched my toast.

'Oh shut up, Sorcha.' He threw me a small smile. 'You know what I mean. And I'm sorry if I've said the wrong thing, my darling.' He kissed Lottie's fingers. 'I didn't mean anything by it. It's a man thing.'

'And sometimes you're a pompous ass,' I said, helpfully.

He laughed and nodded. 'Yes. Sometimes I am.'

I smiled and tapped him on his other hand. 'You're still the best brother in the world though.'

'Thanks. You're not so bad yourself.' He glanced at Lottie. 'You're perfect. In case you are in any doubt. Absolutely perfect, exactly as you are. And I'm glad you don't have a job because if you were still working at that undertakers' business, you wouldn't have come to visit Elsie and we would never have met.'

'I'm glad too. I never liked it there anyway.'

They leaned towards one another and kissed. I buttered another slice of toast, remembering to put the lid back on the butter dish.

'Where does he live?' Asher asked, a minute or so later. 'Finlay Demon, I mean.'

'London.'

I did know that because he'd said so.

'Whereabouts?'

'Oh, I don't know. And I don't know his shoe size, or collar size or anything else. Yet. But I'll be sure to ask when I see him. Just give me a list of questions and I'll go through them one by one.'

'I'm only asking because I care about you and I don't want you to get hurt again.'

I sighed. 'I know. But this time it's different. I admit I've fallen for the wrong men before, but Finlay isn't like any of them. No, really. Don't look at one another like that. Like you've heard it all before. He really is different. You'll see.'

'I'm not trying to upset you, Sorcha, but you've said that before and ... well, that wasn't the case, was it? Take Sean, for example. And before him, there was that awful conman you met at Halloween. Dan. Or Don. Or whatever his name was. If that was even his real name, of course. And prior to him there–'

'Yes. Thank you. We don't need to go through the entire list. And we all remember my ex-husband, I know. I accept all that. But can we give Finlay a chance before we hang, draw and quarter him, please? Yay! Saved by the bell.' I held up my ringing phone so that

Asher could see who was calling. 'It's Finlay. He said he'd call this morning and he's calling. Excuse me please while I take this.'

I jumped up from my chair as I answered the phone, beaming at Asher and Lottie as I darted from the room.

Finlay definitely was The One. He'd even saved me from a lengthy lecture from my brother.

Eight

I was so excited at the prospect of seeing Finlay that I totally forgot I'd already agreed, during the week, to go shopping with Mum, Lottie and Elsie in Easterhill on Saturday afternoon, and that we were then all going to Elsie's for dinner that evening, along with Josie and Diana and their families. Although how we'd all fit around a table in Elsie's cottage was something I couldn't quite work out. Her cottage was probably twice the size of Asher's, but it was still too small to accommodate so many people, in my estimation.

As annoying as it was, I had to call Finlay back and tell him I couldn't meet him owing to some prior commitments that had completely slipped my mind.

I did try to get out of both, or at the very least, one of them, but I knew Asher wouldn't let me off the hook. He'd already made a big deal about how much Lottie was looking forward to our shopping spree and I knew how upset she'd be if I didn't go. And Asher would be livid too, so I couldn't get out of that.

He also pointed out, when I questioned if we'd all fit into Elsie's, that they'd managed perfectly well at Christmas, so he didn't see a problem.

'Ah,' I said, 'But Mum, Dad and I weren't there at Christmas. Will an extra three, fit in?'

True,' he said. 'But Lucy, Kev and Kev's Great Dane, George, were, so yes. An extra three will easily fit in.'

'I seriously hope I'm not the Great Dane in that comparison.' I slapped him on the arm, just in case.

No matter how hard I tried, or what excuse I came up with, Asher had a reason or solution, so in the end I had no choice but to call Finlay and break the bad news.

'Couldn't you meet me at the hotel after dinner?' He sounded almost desperate.

But then again so was I. 'I really wish I could. The problem is that dinner at Elsie's tends to involve rather a lot of alcohol. I won't be in any fit state to walk by 10 p.m. let alone do anything else.'

'You don't have to drink it all, do you?'

I detected a slight irritation in his tone, but he soon laughed, so I must've imagined it.

'It's not a question of just drinking it. Elsie puts it in her food too. I think there's even alcohol in her peanut butter sandwiches.

Hazelnut liqueur, I believe she told me once. Not that we're having sandwiches tonight, so I don't know why I mentioned them. We're having three courses though, so that's a lot of alcohol. Plus the thing with Elsie is that she constantly tops up your glass, so you never know how much you've drunk. Until it's too late.'

'You could say you don't want anything to drink. She can't force it down you.'

I laughed at that. 'If I say I don't want a drink, they'll all know there's something going on, and Asher will give me the third degree, and so will Mum and Dad. But I will try to limit it. Can I call you later? If I can get away, I will. I really want to see you, Finlay. But just like you last night with your friends, I can't simply tell everyone I've now made other plans. And while we're on that subject, I should also mention that I've already promised Asher, Lottie and Mum and Dad that I'll have lunch with them at The Seahorse Inn on Sunday. I can't get out of that either. But Mum and Dad are leaving in the afternoon, so I could get away then, or on Sunday evening. Does that work for you?'

'I suppose it'll have to.'

Now he definitely didn't sound pleased. I probably could've tried to get out of Sunday lunch, but my life wouldn't have been worth living if I did.

Mum, Dad and Asher were of the opinion

that if you made plans with someone you stuck to them unless you had a damn good reason not to.

For me, seeing Finlay was an exceptionally good reason, especially as he and his friends would only be in Seahorse Harbour till Tuesday morning. But I knew, without even asking, that Mum and Asher wouldn't agree. Dad might. But Mum would've soon made him change his mind, and I'd already tried – and failed – to subtly wriggle out of dinner at Elsie's, even though I knew it was a lost cause.

'I'm really sorry, Finlay.'

'Actually, that's perfect,' he said, now sounding far too pleased that I couldn't see him until Sunday night.

'Is it? Are you sure?'

He laughed down the phone. 'Yes. Because it means I can spend today with my mates and not feel guilty for letting either them or you down. Plus, The Seahorse Inn is where we're going for lunch on Sunday. We've already booked it. So that means I can go with them and still see you. It also means I'll get a chance to meet your parents.'

'Meet my parents?' I hoped I didn't sound as horrified as I felt. 'Why would you want to do that?'

'Don't you want me to meet them? If this thing is going anywhere, I'll have to meet them sometime. Why not on Sunday? I had a brief conversation with your dad at the bar last night, although he had no idea I'd fallen head over heels for his daughter at the time. He seemed really nice.'

I was still taking on board the fact that Finlay was saying we had a future together. Which was what he was saying, wasn't it? "If this thing is going anywhere", he'd said.

I'd have preferred it if he'd used the word 'relationship' rather than 'thing', but when a goose has laid you a golden egg, you don't moan because it's not a Fabergé.

'Wait? Did you just say you spoke with my dad?'

'Yes. For about five minutes. What's going on, Sorcha? I'm starting to get the impression you'd rather I hadn't.'

'What? No. I mean, yes. I mean, I'm glad you chatted with him. I'm just surprised, that's all. He's great, don't misunderstand me but Dad's not usually one to chat to strangers. He'd normally just acknowledge any greeting and then look busy so that he can avoid any idle conversation. And yes. I'd love you to meet my parents. I'm just ... well, I'm just surprised you want to. Most men I've been out with would run a mile at the thought of meeting the parents. It's as good as saying, 'let's set the date'. And Mum and Dad can be rather embarrassing. They'll tell you lots of stories about things I did when I was young.'

He chuckled. 'Yeah. Mine would do that too. I can't wait to hear them. And I'm not 'most men', Sorcha. I meant what I said last night. Every word. I've never felt about anyone the way I feel about you. I really think we could have something. I thought you felt the same.'

'I did. I do. I'm just surprised, that's all. If anyone had told me I'd go to my brother's engagement party and fall in love with a gorgeous stranger, I'd have said they were mad.'

I didn't hear what he said in response because suddenly, Nathan bloody Bromley's voice of scorn popped into my head. "Why are you surprised?" he was saying. "You fall in love with every man you meet. For all the good it does you."

'Well, I haven't fallen in love with you,' I muttered.

'You haven't?' Finlay sounded upset.

'I haven't what?'

'You just said you haven't fallen in love with me. I ... I thought last night–'

'I have! I have fallen in love with you. I wasn't talking to ... that is, I didn't mean... Sorry. I was thinking of someone ... something else.'

'Are you sure?'

'Absolutely. One hundred and fifty per cent positive. And I don't care who knows it.'

'I can meet your parents then?'

'Yep. Definitely.'

'So I'll see you at The Seahorse Inn on Sunday, around noon?'

'Yep. I can't wait.'

'I'll have to spend the afternoon with my mates, and possibly some of the evening. But I've been thinking.' He laughed and I was pleased the awkward moment was forgotten. 'I've been thinking of little else if I'm honest. So here it is. I was thinking that, if I booked a room at that posh hotel you mentioned, would you meet me there on Sunday evening?'

I sucked in an excited breath and almost choked on my euphoria.

'I can do that. Mum and Dad will be long gone. I'll find a way to get out of the cottage without Asher asking too many questions.'

'Don't you want him to know about us?'

'I do. But he'll need a little time to get used to it. He doesn't think I should rush in where romance is concerned.'

'He's obviously very protective of you.'

'He is. And I love him for it. He's got me out of ... well, we can talk about all that another time. Oh, Finlay, I can't believe this is happening. All I could think about last night was you.'

That wasn't true. All I could think about last night was bloody Nathan Bromley, but obviously I wasn't going to tell my future husband that.

My. Future. Husband.

Was I moving too fast?

No. He was the one who said we had 'a thing'. A future. Surely that meant marriage?

Okay, maybe not right away, but the way we felt about one another meant it wouldn't be long before we notched things up a peg or two.

And tomorrow night we were going to take the first step towards that.

Tomorrow wasn't just about sex. Tomorrow was about Love. True Love.

And I couldn't wait to rip his clothes off and show him how I felt.

'We could meet for a quick coffee this morning,' I added, now so desperate to see him I couldn't wait until Sunday night.

'This morning? Um. Yeah. I suppose we could. My mates are still asleep, so I could get away for half an hour.'

The prospect didn't seem to thrill him.

'I understand if it's too much of a rush for such a short time. But it would be lovely to see you today, however briefly.'

Did that sound too clingy? Too pathetic? I'm not sure I cared if it did.

'You're right. Coffee would be great. What time and where? Wait. I know. What about that place that woman mentioned last night?'

'Seahorse Bites Café?' I could hear the squeak in my voice.

'Yeah. It's on the promenade, isn't it? I'll

meet you there at 10, if that's good for you. I haven't had breakfast yet, have you?'

'I have. Sorry. But I could eat some more toast.' I glanced at my watch. 'Wait. It's 9.45 now!'

'Yep. See you very soon, Sorcha.'

He'd rung off before I had time to explain that fifteen minutes wasn't enough time to make myself look stunning. Especially not first thing in the morning. Although I had been up since 8, and I'd showered and dressed before breakfast.

I could slap on some make-up and quickly change my clothes. I might be a few minutes late, but at least I'd get to see Finlay today.

Nine

I don't know why, but Asher made a bit of a fuss about me nipping out to see Finlay. I wished I hadn't told him. I definitely wouldn't be telling him about our plans for Sunday night. Or even Sunday lunch.

'What's the big deal?' I asked. 'It's just a cup of coffee. We're not running off to Gretna Green or anything.'

'Funny.' He wasn't smiling. 'I just don't want you to rush into anything.'

'I repeat. It's a cup of coffee. Not a wedding ceremony. See you later, Lottie.'

'Have fun,' she called out from the kitchen, and Merry also gave a loud bark of encouragement. At least that's what I took it to be.

I grabbed my coat from the rack in the hall and Asher followed me towards the front door.

'Thankfully, you can't just turn up somewhere and get married, these days. Not even at Gretna Green, in case you were thinking about it.' He threw me a tiny grin before resuming the lecture. 'You only met the guy last night, Sorcha.'

I tutted. 'Yes. And I'm meeting him again today. That's how dating works.'

'Dating? So you're dating him?'

I sighed as loudly and as dramatically as I could.

'I'm getting to know him better. I can go through that list of questions, if you'd like.' I heard the clock in the sitting room strike the hour. 'And now I'm late. Thanks. See you later. Don't do anything I wouldn't do.'

I kissed him on the cheek, yanked the door open, and closed it behind me before he had time to say anything else.

But I did reopen it to add, 'Is Gretna Green far?' Quickly closing it again as a look of horror swept across his face.

I know I shouldn't, but sometimes I just can't help winding him up. Especially when I'm feeling happy.

And I was feeling ecstatic. I was seeing Finlay Demon again, and I really couldn't wait.

I'd changed my jeans for a black fitted skirt and knee-length black boots, and my scruffy but comfy sweater for a baby-blue cashmere one. I soon regretted that. It was a gloriously sunny morning, but it was absolutely freezing. Brass monkeys wouldn't even venture out on a day like this. The wind was biting.

I lowered my head to avoid dust, sand and other bits of debris flying into my eyes but my hair whipped my face and tied itself in tangles.

I never run, but I picked up my pace and reached Sea Walk in seconds.

The wind was worse on the promenade, being an onshore wind coming directly off the sea, and with my hair now blown across my face like some sort of netting, I couldn't see much at all.

I thought I'd crashed into the side wall of Beach Bakers when I turned left, but there was a bit of give, plus it smelled far too nice for a wall, and it also said, 'Oof!' and 'Bloody hell, Sorcha!' So I knew it wasn't a wall.

I realised immediately who it was.

Nathan bloody Bromley.

'Sorry! But it wasn't my fault. I couldn't see a thing.'

I tried to untangle my hair but I think I was just making it worse.

'Let me do it.'

He stepped in front of me to shelter me from the worst of the wind, and I could feel his fingers gently weaving through the mass of tangles. A couple of times I flinched when his hands brushed against my face.

Okay, perhaps flinched isn't quite the right word. Perhaps I should say I tensed. All I know is I felt something strange. Not bad, exactly, but definitely odd. I was very glad when he finished, that much I can say for certain.

'All done,' he said. 'I hope I didn't hurt you too much. I could feel you jump a few times.'

'Thanks. No. You...' I looked up at his face and the concern ... and something else in his eyes, almost took my breath away for a second. 'You didn't hurt me.'

He cleared his throat and stuffed his hands in his coat pockets. I kept mine on my hair, firmly holding it in place.

'Where are you going in such a hurry?'

'Oh. Er. To the café.'

Something lit up his eyes making them seem brighter and even more intense than usual.

'The café?'

'Yes. I'm meeting Finlay for coffee. He's the guy from last night in case you've for–'

'I haven't forgotten him.'

'Er. Well I'm already late, so I must dash. Thanks again for untangling my hair.'

'Anytime.' His smile looked forced as he stepped aside. The wind hit me full in the face once more and as my hair fought for freedom, I struggled to keep it in check.

'Aren't you going back in?' I nodded in the direction of the café.

'Later. I'm on my way to The Olde Forge. Liam's been making something for Lyn, and last night he said I could collect it this morning. I thought I'd pop out after the initial rush for breakfasts.' He frowned suddenly. 'The guy's not in there.'

'What?' He must've noticed me peering towards the café.

'Finlay. He isn't in the café.'

I didn't mean to, but I glanced at my watch, and several strands of hair lashed my face.

'He must be running late,' I said, tugging them back under control.

'Did you make a definite arrangement to meet up?'

'Yes. We did. I already told you. And it's called a date, Nathan. Not an arrangement.'

I don't know why I said that. I saw him tense, and tighten his jaw, but concern soon filled his eyes and his voice was compassionate – even though his words were not.

'Perhaps he's not coming, Sorcha. Perhaps something else has come up. Or he's changed his mind.'

I laughed. Possibly a little hysterically. And I know I snapped at him in response.

'We arranged it less than half an hour ago, so I doubt that very much.'

He shrugged. 'You know better than most that sometimes men say they'll do something, which they have no intention of doing.'

'What does that mean? No! Don't bother trying to explain. I know exactly what you meant. You can be so mean, sometimes.'

'I'm really sorry. I don't aim to be. I'm just

being truthful. I never seem to say the right thing to you.'

'Well. For your information, women do that too. Say they'll do things they don't intend to do. Like, I could say I'd go on a date with you, for example. But I'd never, ever do that.'

His eyes narrowed a fraction. 'I haven't asked you on a date.'

'I'm well aware of that. It was merely an example.'

He furrowed his brows. 'I don't see how that...'

His voice trailed off and I followed the direction of his gaze.

'Finlay!'

I was so pleased to see Finlay walking towards us that I let go of my hair and hurried to meet him.

The wind whipped it up into a whirling frenzy and I probably resembled Medusa ... on cocaine or something.

Which is definitely not how I wanted to look when Finlay saw me again.

Ten

'I look a mess,' I said, untangling my hair again as Finlay and I sat at one of the tables in the window after ordering two coffees from Lyn.

'You look lovely.' He didn't offer to help. He rested his forearms on the table and glanced towards the sea. 'I'm glad I'm not out on a boat today.'

'Ow.' I got the last knot out and stared at the rough and choppy sea. It was crashing over the rocks and the swash was rushing up the sand and coming within metres of the foot of the raised promenade. Once or twice over the years, during a severe storm, seawater has topped the promenade and made it as far up as the doors of the shops on Sea Walk. But thankfully that wouldn't be happening today. No storms were forecast. Just very windy weather. 'Yeah. I'm glad I'm not a seahorse. They'll be out in deeper water, no doubt, as the weather today will probably be churning up the seagrass. Although the cliffs offer some protection to The Shallows. The onshore wind is whipping up waves and stirring up the seabed resulting in that sludge-coloured water.'

He turned to look at me with the hint of a smile on his mouth as he raised his brows.

'Do you know a lot about the sea?'

'Not really. But Asher's a Seahorse Rider, so he's taught me some stuff.'

'A Seahorse Rider?' Now he was laughing. 'You're not seriously telling me that he tries to ride seahorses, are you? Aren't they tiny little things?'

I grinned. 'A Seahorse Rider is what they call the volunteers in Seahorse Harbour who help to look after the seahorses. And seahorses can be as tiny as this.' I picked a small piece of brown rock crystal sugar from the bowl Lyn had placed on our table with our coffees. 'About 1.5 centimetres. To as big as your foot, depending on the species.' I popped the sugar crystal in my mouth and crunched it.

Finlay grinned back. 'I hope you're not planning on doing that with my foot.'

I laughed, and then leaned forward and tried to look, and sound, sexy.

'No. But I can think of a few things I'd like to do with your foot.'

On reflection, it didn't come across as that sexy, but Finlay gave me a totally devilish grin, and winked at me, so it must've sounded okay to him.

'Sorcha?'

'Yes Finlay.'

He reached out and took my fingers in his, twisting and entwining them for a second or two.

'What's the situation with you and that guy, Nathan?'

The question took me completely by surprise and I blinked a few times before I answered.

'Situation? There isn't one. We're friends. Although we're not even that, really. We're not close or anything. Why do you ask?'

He smiled and shrugged.

'There was just something about the way he looked at you when I arrived. I thought, perhaps, you might've dated in the past. Or maybe would in the future.'

'Me and Nathan, date?' I shook my head. 'No way. Nah-uh.'

'Don't you find him attractive?'

'Nope. Not in the least? Are you jealous? You don't have any cause to be. Besides. I thought I made my feelings clear. The only person I want in my future, is you.'

The smile grew wider. He raised our entwined fingers and planted a soft kiss on mine.

'Good. I ... Damn.' He took his ringing phone from his jeans and the smile disappeared as he glared at the screen as if he didn't want to answer it.

'Are you okay? Is it your friends chasing you?'

I forced a smile and hoped he could stay for longer.

'Sorry. I've got to take this.'

He let go of my hand, shot upright and dashed towards the door, glancing at me over his shoulder with what I can only describe as a fearful look in his eyes.

He almost crashed headlong into Nathan who was returning from Liam's pottery carrying a large and heavy-looking object.

'Don't you dare say a word,' I said, as Nathan opened his mouth to speak and the bell above the door tinkled as the door swung shut behind Finlay's back.

'I wasn't going to,' Nathan said, bending to place the object on the floor, just to one side of the entrance. 'Lyn! I'm back.'

Lyn hurried out from the kitchen, wiping her hands on a towel, and beaming at Nathan.

'Let me see it then,' she said, her voice heavy with excitement. 'You unwrap it. My hands are still wet.'

Nathan unwrapped the object and I darted my gaze from that to Finlay, who was pacing up and down outside speaking animatedly into his phone. He caught my eye and quickly looked away.

Something twisted in my tummy so I gave my full attention to the object again.

As Nathan tore off more wrapping, a large and beautiful, ceramic seahorse was revealed. It gleamed in the sunshine pouring through the window and almost looked like it was made of gold and bronze and silver, but there was also a subtle kaleidoscope of other colours running through it. Purples and greens and reds. It was truly amazing.

'Oh wow!' I said. 'That's gorgeous, Lyn. Liam's so talented. Is it for here or for your home?'

Lyn had tears in her eyes as she pulled Nathan towards her by his coat collar and planted a big, sloppy and rather noisy, kiss on his cheek.

'You're the best nephew in the world,' she said, wiping away the red lip imprint on his cheek with her thumb, before beaming at me. 'It's for here. Nathan had it made for me. Isn't he a treasure? It was supposed to be a surprise, but Orla let it slip at the engagement party last night and I've been like a teapot waiting for the kettle to boil all morning. It's got to have pride of place.'

She glanced around the café, gently stroking the seahorse's coronet with one hand and tapping her chin with the other.

'That was really good of you,' I said, lowering my voice and jokingly whispering,

'It's not Lyn's birthday or something is it? I'd hate to have missed getting her a card.'

He grinned at me and so did Lyn.

'It's not,' she said. 'And I really don't deserve such a beautiful gift.' She linked her arm through his. 'I'm so lucky to have you.'

'I'm the lucky one,' he said. 'And you deserve a lot more than a ceramic seahorse.'

The other customers in the café all made lovely comments. One or two even asked where Nathan had got it. He handed out some of Liam's cards and gave a young couple, directions to the pottery, which was only a few minutes away, opposite the church.

'Over there,' Lyn said, pointing to a shelf near the counter and the till. 'I can see it from in here and also from the kitchen, so that's the perfect place.' She hurried over to the shelf and wiped it with the towel she was holding.

Nathan bent down to lift the seahorse and as he met my eye, he nodded his head in Finlay's direction.

'Is everything okay?'

'Yes, of course,' I said, in a high-pitched tone. I cleared my throat. 'Why wouldn't it be?'

'I don't know.' He stood upright; the seahorse nestled in his arms. 'He's been out there for a while and he doesn't look exactly happy. I hope it's not bad news.'

'Bad news for me, you mean? You think that's his wife calling, or another girlfriend, don't you? You think he's like all the rest.'

'Whoa! I didn't mean anything of the sort. I think that's on you, Sorcha. Is that who you think he's talking to? A wife or another girlfriend?'

'No! Absolutely not. You'd better look where you're going or you'll trip up and break that.'

He hesitated for a second as if he had more to say, but he sighed and moved away, gently placing the seahorse in position and moving it back and forth and an inch here and there until Lyn declared she was happy.

I was glad someone was.

Nathan was right. Finlay didn't look happy.

And neither was I.

And he was also right about what I was thinking. And I couldn't wait for Finlay to come back inside so that I could interrogate him about it.

Eleven

'I don't have a wife, or another girlfriend.' Finlay wasn't pleased about my questions. 'That was ... just a guy I know. Someone I said I'd do something for. But I think I'm beginning to wish I hadn't, that's all.'

'Oh. I'm sorry, Finlay. But you must be able to see why I was concerned. You seemed really worried and you dashed outside and paced around for ages. And you looked ... guilty somehow. As if you were trying to hide something.'

'Guilty? I've got nothing to feel guilty about. And I told you last night that I was single.'

'Er. I'm not sure you did. You just said you haven't been in love for a while.'

'Okay, fine. I'm telling you now. I'm single.'

'Okay. I'm sorry.'

He puffed out a breath, leaned forward and took my hands in his.

'No. I'm the one who should be sorry. I

didn't mean to snap at you like that. But your questions took me by surprise. And so did that phone call.' He sighed softly. 'Actually, I did lie just now.'

I shot a look at his face. 'You did?'

I tried to snatch my hands away but he held them firmly in his as he nodded, grinning all the while.

'Uh-huh. I said I didn't have a girlfriend, and I do. You.'

'Me?'

'Yes, you. Unless you don't want the part.'

'I do!' I leaned forward to meet him and our faces were just inches apart. 'I really do.'

I thought he was going to kiss me, but he leaned back against the seat, now loosely holding just one hand.

'Good.' He smiled at me before glancing at the clock on the wall opposite. 'Oh hell. I've got to go.'

He stood up so fast I almost got whiplash in my neck, watching him.

'I'll walk with you.' I stood up and grabbed my coat from the back of the chair.

'I think your friend might want a word with you.'

He nodded his head towards the counter where I could see Nathan was loitering, trying to look busy, while Lyn admired her seahorse from every possible angle, and took photos of it on her phone.

I lowered my voice. 'I told you. We're not really friends. And right now, there's nothing he could say that I want to hear. I'd rather spend a few more minutes with you.'

'That sounds good to me.'

I shrugged on my coat as he took some cash from his jeans and left enough to pay for our coffees and for a fairly generous tip. I like a man who tips well. It shows he's not mean where money is concerned.

'Bye, Nathan. Bye, Lyn.' I called out.

'Cheerio, Love,' Lyn said. 'Don't be a stranger.'

'See you soon, I hope,' Nathan said, looking like he wanted to say a lot more.

The wind was still biting but it had subsided quite a bit. Now my hair just danced around my shoulders as we walked along Sea Walk. I was hoping Finlay would hold my hand again but he stopped a few seconds after we left the café and grinned at me.

'I'm going that way.' He pointed towards Seahorse Harbour Holiday Park, which was just along the promenade from where we stood outside Beach Bakers.

'Oh. Er. I'm going this way, I suppose.' I pointed up Church Hill. 'You can see Asher's cottage from here. It's that pink one. On the end of Rope Way.'

He tilted his head a fraction. The cottage was only a few hundred yards away.

'Very nice. Pink's a surprising colour, having met Asher.'

'It was pink when he bought it. It doesn't seem to bother him. I think he likes it.'

'Right. I'll see you tomorrow then.'

'Um. Yes. Okay. Finlay? Are you still cross with me about my suspicions?'

He frowned. 'No.'

'Then is it something else I've said or done?'

'Er. I'm not following you.'

'You seem ... distracted. Distant. You weren't like this last night. Or earlier. You do still want to see me, don't you?'

'Of course I do.' He stepped closer. 'You have no idea how much I want to see you.'

'There's no one around. You could ... kiss me, if you like.'

His brows shot up a fraction. He stepped even closer and looked me in the eye.

'On the street? I could. And believe me, I really want to. But there's just one problem. If I did, I'd have to go and take a very long and a very cold shower. And then I'd have to take several more as I wouldn't be able to stop thinking about kissing you. And touching you. And making love to you. Today, tonight and tomorrow, would be torture. I'd rather wait until tomorrow night, wouldn't you? When I can kiss you all over your body, without having to stop, and without fear of your brother or anyone else getting in the way.'

'I … I suppose you're right. I wouldn't be able to concentrate on anything Lottie, Mum or Elsie said today, or this evening. And the thought of tomorrow is so exciting. But I do want to kiss you, Finlay. I really do.'

'Same here.' He gave me a quick peck on my cheek and sent a rush of emotion coursing through me. 'But tomorrow will be wonderful. Just you wait and see. Have fun today. I'll call you later to say goodnight.'

I watched him go and I must admit, I was confused.

If kissing me and having to walk away, would be torture, why wasn't *not* kissing me, torture too?

I definitely felt as if I was being starved, or something. Tormented in some way.

And the annoying thing was, I knew I wouldn't be able to get that out of my head for the rest of the day.

Why was kissing me far worse than not kissing me?

I was pretty sure Nathan Bromley would have a thing or two to say about that.

But there was no way I was ever going to ask him.

Twelve

Needless to say, I spent most of the afternoon mulling over that kiss. Or I suppose I should say, the no kiss.

I really couldn't understand it. Finlay either loved me or he didn't. And if he loved me, surely he'd want to kiss me as often as possible, wouldn't he?

But then again, wasn't the first kiss the one that should be really special? Standing on the promenade on a blustery February morning, wasn't that romantic, was it?

Perhaps Finlay was right. Waiting until we were somewhere private meant that we could take our time. Luxuriate in that kiss. Prolong the moment for as long as possible.

And then we could slowly explore one another's bodies and make love all night.

That was much better than a kiss on the promenade, knowing we'd have to wait to take things further.

Now I understood.

And I needed to buy some extremely sexy underwear.

I managed to sneak away from Lottie, Mum and Elsie, on the pretext of needing the loo. But unbeknown to me, Mum had decided she needed the loo too, and had followed me.

'Are you sure there's a Ladies toilet on this floor?' Mum said, making me jump as I scanned the lingerie section of the only remaining department store in Easterhill. 'Why are you looking at lingerie?'

'Er. Because I'm buying some for Lottie as a present.'

'Lingerie?'

'Yes.'

'Do you usually buy your friends underwear as presents?'

'Yes.'

I never had, but Mum wouldn't know that.

She shrugged. 'I don't think that's her size.'

I forgot I was holding a black lace bra and matching knickers.

'It is. I checked before we came out.'

'You went through Lottie's knicker-drawer?'

'Er. No. I found some in the clean laundry basket, waiting to be ironed.'

'Lottie irons her underwear? I'm impressed. I didn't think you girls did that these days. Mind you, there's hardly enough material to iron on that set you're holding. And

I'm really not convinced it is the right size. It looks more your size.'

'Well it's Lottie's size. Okay? And besides, we're about the same size anyway.'

'Really cherub? Hmm. I'm not sure about that. But if you say you've checked then I'm sure you have. Now where, exactly, is the Ladies room?'

'It's near the restaurant on the third floor.'

'But we were in the restaurant on the third floor having coffee. Why did you bring me down here?'

'I didn't, Mum. You followed me. But I wanted to buy this lingerie.'

'So you didn't need the loo?'

'No. And I don't need this conversation either. Go back the way you came and turn left when you reach the restaurant. The loo is right there. I'll see you back in the restaurant in half an hour.'

'It won't take half an hour to buy those.'

I sighed. 'I know. But I want to buy a dress as well.'

'For Lottie? That's very generous of you.'

'For me, Mum. I'm buying a dress for myself.'

'Oh, I see. Well why don't I come with you?'

'I thought you needed to pee.'

'Oh yes. I knew there was something I wanted to do. Menopause is no fun, cherub. You wait and see. I'll be forgetting my own name before long.'

I watched her go and cursed under my breath. Now I'd have to buy Lottie some underwear in case Mum ever mentioned it. And that felt a bit weird, to be honest. I didn't have a clue what sort of underwear she liked. Or whether she'd appreciate getting some from me.

I'd get her the sexiest and scantiest I could find, and tell her it was a joke present from me, Josie and Diana.

And I'd get myself the same, for my rendezvous with Finlay.

Having done that, it didn't take long to find the perfect dress. I saw it on a mannequin as I left the lingerie section. It was a deep, dark blue, slim fitting mini with a twist knot halter neck and a low and tantalisingly revealing cut-out detail to the front, and a plunging V-shaped back. Thankfully they had it in my size. I bought a new pair of high heeled, over the knee, suede boots as well. They looked incredibly sexy and tied at the top with a bow lace and I swear they whistled to me as I walked through the footwear section. Or maybe I whistled at them.

Now I really couldn't wait for Sunday night.

But first I had to get through Saturday night at Elsie's. And I already had a headache just thinking about that.

Elsie's really lovely and she's great fun too. Lottie's really lucky to have her for her mum. Although I'm not sure I would've been as quick as Lottie was to forgive her. But then Lottie's such a lovely, kind-hearted person.

But any occasion with Elsie tends to be loud, packed with people, overflowing with alcohol and involve a lot of dancing. Elsie loves to dance. Even our shopping spree ended with us doing a Tango at a Spanish restaurant where we'd stopped for a quick glass of wine and some tapas before getting a cab home. By the time we left, several glasses of wine later, the entire clientele of the restaurant had joined in and Elsie was dancing on the bar.

To be honest, I can't remember much about the evening at Elsie's. Only that it was packed, loud, I got drunk, and we all ended up dancing. Including Dad, and also, Alex.

The walk – or I should say stagger – back to Asher's sobered me up and I was tempted to call Finlay and tell him I'd meet him at the hotel, if he could get a room. But I decided I was still a bit too inebriated. I wanted our night together to be wonderful and me getting hiccups, which I often did when drunk, wouldn't bode well for that.

He did call me, as he promised, and we chatted for a while, but I think I fell asleep before we actually said goodnight.

Thirteen

'Did you know he was going to be here?'

Asher didn't look pleased when we walked into The Seahorse Inn on Sunday and saw Finlay and his friends.

For a man who is deeply in love and has just got engaged to the woman of his dreams, Asher seemed to be spending an inordinate amount of time asking me questions about Finlay Demon.

'He mentioned it. Yes. But as we were already coming here I don't think that's relevant.'

'But it is a coincidence.'

'Oh Ash, for pity's sake, get over yourself. Seahorse Harbour is tiny, and this is the only pub in the village. They're staying at the Seahorse Harbour Holiday Park, which as you know, only has Pool Pizzas, Happy Hot Dogs and Ice Dreams. Although Ice Dreams only serves ice cream and it's not open in the winter. None serve Sunday lunch. They're here for a bachelor's weekend so they would hardly go to Hippocampus for an à la carte lunch, would they? The pub is the obvious place they would be.'

I tutted loudly for emphasis and Asher scowled at me.

'I suppose so. Just be careful, Sorcha. That's all I ask.'

'You know me,' I replied in a sing-song voice.

'Precisely. That's the problem.'

I let out a loud and rather childish sigh, blowing a raspberry at him and screwing up my face.

'One day I might surprise you.'

'That doesn't fill me with confidence.'

He grinned at me though and gently nudged my arm.

I waved at Finlay and he waved back, mouthing the words, 'I'll see you soon.' At least I think that's what he said. I'm rubbish at lip reading.

Lottie, Asher and I made our way to the table in one of the window spots, where Mum and Dad were already waiting, a glass of white wine in front of Mum and a large whisky in front of Dad.

'How are we all this morning?' Mum asked, beaming at us and patting the chair beside her. 'Come and sit beside me, Lottie.'

'It's the afternoon,' I said. 'But I'm feeling

wonderful, thanks. How are you two doing?'

Mum chuckled. 'We're fine. But goodness me, I'd forgotten what a gossip Lilith Shoe is.' She shook her head and tutted. 'I didn't think I'd ever manage to get away. In the end your father told her, in a rather abrupt manner, we had to go or we'd be late. But it was still another ten minutes before I could get to the front door.'

'So what's the gossip then?' I asked. 'I suppose she had plenty to say about Alex and Diana's little drama on Friday night.'

Mum nodded and took a sip of wine. Dad rolled his eyes and shook his head.

'You know better than most, baby girl, that your mother and I take no notice of tittle tattle.'

'Please don't call me baby girl, Dad. I'm almost thirty-four.'

'That's as maybe, but you'll always be my baby girl.'

'Unless Mum ever has another baby.' I couldn't help myself.

Dad made some strange noise between a cough and a splutter and Mum went beetroot and emptied the contents of her glass.

'No thank you, cherub. Two was quite enough for me.'

I saw Asher grin and shake his head at me and I wondered for the umpteenth time why it was that they never call him anything other than Asher.

With me it's always, baby girl, or cherub, or little one. I especially hate little one.

I think they do it on purpose to irritate me, but Asher assures me they do it because they adore me.

I accept that's probably true, but it doesn't alter the fact that cute names and tags are for babies and children, not for grown women of my age. Unless of course, they're said by a hot man – like Finlay Demon. He can call me baby girl, or cherub, or even, at a push, little one. In fact, he can call me anything he wants. On the whole, I'd prefer him to call me Sexy Sorcha, or something including the word 'sexy', or 'hot' or ... You get the picture.

'What's everyone having to drink?' Dad asked, getting up from his seat and neatly changing the subject.

'I'll have another white wine, darling,' Mum said.

'Me too, Dad. Large please.'

'Lottie?' Asher smiled at his fiancée. 'Are you having white wine too?'

'Yes please.'

'I'll give you a hand, Dad,' Asher said, placing a hand on Dad's back as they headed for the bar.

The Seahorse Inn looks like one of those olde worlde pubs from the outside, but inside it's a mish-mash of various eras and styles. It's got heavy, black beams across the ceiling and staggered in several places on the walls. There's a large fireplace in the far wall and at this time of year the tables closest to it are the ones that get taken first.

Mum doesn't like sitting too close to the fire, so our table was on the opposite side of the pub, in front of one of the windows. She says it gives you thread veins in your cheeks. I thought that was from too much alcohol or spicy food, or maybe that's something else. I can't recall.

Even from here though, you can feel the warmth from the flames. Or perhaps that's the central heating.

The white-washed walls are hung with ropes, nets and other fishing paraphernalia, more of which hangs from the black beams across the low, white-washed ceiling.

Photographs of Seahorse Harbour from days of old right up to the present time, together with paintings of the sea, seahorses, or ships are displayed higgledy-piggledy around the walls.

There are also several ceramic seahorses on the large window sills, most of which were made by Liam Fulbright, Josie's partner.

The whole thing produces a somewhat eclectic look. But if I did this in my room, most people would just call it a mess. And yet this place feels cosy and welcoming.

It also helps that it's owned by Mikkel Meloy, the man who looks like a hot Viking, only better.

But not as good as Finlay.

I stretched my neck, and strained to see him now that I was sitting down, but the throng of customers gave an impenetrable view. Mum and Lottie were chatting about how wonderful the party had been on Friday, and how much fun we had shopping in Easterhill on Saturday, and then at Elsie's that evening. I smiled and nodded at the appropriate times.

'We must do this again soon,' Mum enthused.

'I'd love that,' Lottie said, beaming so hard that I'm sure she actually glowed.

'Yeah. That'd be great,' I said. 'I can't wait.'

I thought I heard Finlay laugh, for a second. I might've imagined that.

I almost laughed when I heard Mum's next sentence and saw the expression on Lottie's face.

'Now that you and Asher are engaged, you must call me Mum. But only if you're comfortable doing so. I know you've lost your mum, and have just discovered your real mum, so perhaps you'd rather not have someone else you're calling mum. But I was thinking about it last night, and I'd really like it. If you're happy to, that is.'

'Er. Thank you,' Lottie said. 'I'd be very happy to call you mum ... Mum. Assuming that's okay with Asher.'

'Assuming what's okay with me?' Asher smiled at Lottie as he and Dad returned to the table, laden with drinks and each carrying a couple of menus under their arms.

'That Lottie calls me Mum.'

Asher seemed surprised but delighted, even though his question had been directed at his fiancée.

'That's fine by me,' he said. 'It's more than fine. It's perfect.'

'You haven't mentioned it,' Mum said, 'but I've got to ask. Have you set the date yet? I thought you might discuss it last night at Elsie's, but you didn't, and it wasn't my place to bring it up.'

'You're bringing it up now,' I said.

'Because we're going home this afternoon, and I wondered if there was anything we should chat about face to face.'

'The date?' Asher glanced at Lottie. 'You mean the wedding date?'

'Of course I mean the wedding date.' Mum laughed.

Lottie shook her head. 'Not yet. We've discussed it a bit, and we'd like to make it soon, but we haven't decided on a date.'

'We're thinking about June,' Asher added. 'But it's the height of the tourist season.'

Mum frowned. 'What difference does that make?'

'A lot.' Asher tutted. 'You know I'm a

member of The Seahorse Riders and I've told you many times that the summer months are our busiest period. With all the tourists going in and out of the water, swimming, sailing, using boards and sometimes even jet skis, it takes all of us to make sure the seahorses are kept safe. And there's not that many of us. Although I'm hoping Nathan will join us soon.'

I choked on my wine. 'Nathan? Nathan Bromley? A Seahorse Rider?'

Asher frowned at me. 'Yes. Why does that surprise you? He's a strong swimmer. He knows how to sail, surf, dive and just about anything else on, in and under the sea. He understands the weather and the tides. He cares about the seahorses as much as Lyn does. And he's good with people.'

'Good with people? I'm not sure about that.'

'Of course he is,' Asher said. 'I don't know why you seem to have it in for him. But anyway. We were discussing the wedding.'

'I'm happy to wait until the autumn,' Lottie said, half to Asher and half to Mum, after smiling apologetically at me.

'What about a winter wedding?' I suggested, trying to get into the spirit of it and get Nathan Bromley off my mind. Good with people! Huh. 'Or even better, a Christmas wedding.'

Asher pulled a face. 'Yeah, right. And what

if the weather this Christmas turns out like it did last Christmas? You, Mum and Dad couldn't get here due to the blizzards.'

'But wouldn't a Christmas wedding be wonderful?' Lottie looked all dreamy-eyed. 'Especially as we met just before Christmas. We could get married on the anniversary of our first meeting. That would be so romantic.'

'It would also be extremely cold,' Mum said. 'No bride wants to walk down the aisle shivering in her bridal gown.'

'Unless it's with excitement,' I quipped.

'I'll definitely be excited,' Lottie said.

'You'll be a nervous wreck.' Dad patted Asher on the back. 'I know I was.'

Mum stared at him, wide-eyed. 'You've never told me that. What did you have to be nervous about?'

'The wedding night?' I offered, and immediately wished I hadn't.

'Oh cherub, don't be silly.' Mum tutted and laughed. 'It wasn't as if it was our first time. Don't look at me like that. Our generation had sex before marriage too, you know.'

'Thanks for sharing,' Asher said, rolling his eyes at me and avoiding looking at Mum.

'You don't buy a car without testing how it drives,' Mum said.

Dad raised his brows. 'If I'd said that, you'd have given me a clip round the ear.'

Mum laughed louder and blew him a kiss.

'I need the loo.' I got up and headed in that general direction.

I didn't need the loo. I wanted to see Finlay.

'I was just about to come over and say hi,' he said, as I neared the table where he and his friends sat by the fire.

'Mum and Dad are talking about sex. I thought I'd get away for a few minutes.'

'Are they?' He laughed and reached out his hand to me. 'Don't you like talking about sex?'

'Yes. But not about my parents having it.'

'Ah. I see. You must have very open-minded parents. My parents would never discuss their sex life in front of me.'

'Nor would mine. Normally. Perhaps Asher getting engaged has made them feel old, and they're trying to relive their youth or something.'

He pulled me gently onto his lap and I sat down with one arm draped around his shoulder. Last night when he called me and we had a chat, he'd completely reassured me about his feelings. He'd explained that not kissing me on Saturday morning was as much of a torture as kissing me would've been, and that he'd realised he was an idiot and would make it up to me. I can't remember what else he said, because, as I mentioned, I think I nodded off, but I was genuinely happy to see him today.

'Hello you,' Andy said. 'I've forgotten your

name. I'm Andy. And I can be very 'andy, if you know what I mean.'

He winked and stuck his tongue out at the side of his mouth in what was probably supposed to be an amusing gesture, but wasn't.

'I'll bear that in mind. My name's Sorcha.'

'Is that foreign? It sounds foreign. But you don't. You sound posh.'

I laughed. 'I'm neither posh nor foreign.'

'Just gorgeous,' Finlay whispered in my ear, sending shivers up and down my spine.

'Well, any friend of Finlay's is a friend of ours. Isn't that right?' Andy held up his beer glass and glanced at the group of friends around the table.

'That's right,' they all said in unison, clinking glasses and cheering loudly.

'Are they drunk again?' I asked as quietly as I could.

Finlay grinned. 'Not again. They're still drunk from last night. And probably still from Friday night, too. They're merely topping themselves up.'

'But not you?'

He shook his head. 'I prefer to keep my wits about me. I got seriously drunk once, a long time ago, and I vowed I would never do it again. Apart from a hangover that I swear lasted for at least a week, I did something really stupid. I'm still paying the price for that. I'll never put myself in that position again.'

'Oh? That sounds serious. What happened?'

He looked almost startled. As if he hadn't meant to say that. He diverted his gaze to the fire and slowly shook his head.

'It's not something I like to talk about, and this isn't the time or place. I don't know why I mentioned it.' He met my eyes and smiled. 'Don't worry. It's nothing illegal. Just deeply personal. I'll tell you one day. But not today. Sorry.'

'That's okay. I understand.'

I didn't. And of course, now I really wanted to know what it was that Finlay had done that was so bad that he never got drunk again.

Fourteen

I had been a bit nervous about introducing Finlay to my parents, even though Finlay had already told me he had chatted with Dad for a while at the engagement party. But I needn't have worried at all. Finlay was the embodiment of every parents' perfect boyfriend for their offspring. I think he could charm the birds from the trees.

Even Asher had warmed to him by the time we all finished lunch, and Lottie told me, when she and I both nipped to the loo together, that, like me, she genuinely believed Finlay might actually be The One.

I laughed ecstatically. 'I was beginning to doubt he existed. I thought I was doomed to either spend my life alone, or with a stream of utter bastards. Or dick-heads at the very least.'

'And to think, only last week you were broken-hearted over Sean. Along comes Finlay Demon and suddenly everything has changed!'

If anyone other than Lottie had made that

comment, I might have thought they were being facetious. It was the sort of thing Nathan Bromley would say. But although I didn't know Lottie that well, I knew she had a heart of gold and that she didn't mean anything derogatory by it. She was clearly happy for me. And she was almost as excited as I was when I told her of our plans for later.

'You're going to stay at the Easterhill Hotel tonight? Oh wow. Does Asher know?'

'Er. No. And I know I shouldn't ask you this, but please don't tell him, Lottie.'

'You want me to lie to him? I'm not sure I can do that, Sorcha.'

'No. Not lie. Just don't tell him.'

'But what if he asks me if I know where you are?'

I grinned mischievously.

'I need you to use your womanly wiles.'

'My what?' She laughed. 'I'm not sure I have those.'

'Of course you do. Asher's crazy about you. All I need you to do is persuade him to have an early night. I'll offer to take Merry out for a walk before bed – which I'll do. And then I'll bring her home, make sure she's settled for the night, and sneak out again without Asher knowing.'

'That might work. But what if he hears you?'

'I'll be as silent as the grave.'

'And what about tomorrow morning?'

'I'll get back before he's up.'

'Are you sure? You know how early he gets up to go running.'

I grinned at her again. 'You could persuade him to stay in bed.'

She laughed suddenly. 'I think you're confusing me with someone else. I'm hardly a sex goddess or anything.'

'You are to Asher. Believe me. If you give him a choice between going running or staying in bed and having morning sex, I can guarantee which one he'll choose. Most men would. And if you wear that lingerie we gave you last night, Asher will want to stay in bed all day.'

I'd taken Josie and Diana aside at Elsie's and told them that I'd bought Lottie a joke present but that I wanted it to be from the three of us. They both agreed and they even offered to pay me for their share. I declined the offer. I was just grateful the underwear wasn't going to be solely from me.

We gave it to Lottie in the kitchen so that no one else would see it. Including Asher. But Mum came in and saw us and stayed while Lottie opened it.

'Is it your size?' Mum asked.

'Yes it is.' Lottie was thrilled.

Mum seemed surprised. But then she didn't know the set she'd seen me holding in the store, was for me, and I'd got another size for Lottie, having called Asher to ask him to go and look in Lottie's knicker-drawer for me.

I don't know. The things we have to do for Love. I do seem to get myself into some awkward situations.

'Why?' Asher had asked.

'Because we're getting her some joke undies.'

'Joke undies? What are those? They don't make fart noises or something do they? I'm not sure Lottie would like that.'

'No they don't. Don't worry about it, Asher. Just go and check her size, will you?'

'I'm just about to neuter a cat.'

'Ew! Thanks for sharing. Male or female?'

'Male. Does that matter?'

'It does to the cat. I'm sure he won't mind if you delay that for a few minutes.'

'Can't you wait?'

'No, Ash. I can't. Just run upstairs and look. It'll take you less than two minutes. And then you can castrate that poor cat.'

Thankfully, he did as I asked.

And now Lottie was still laughing as she shook her head. 'Okay. I'll give it a try. But only because I love him so much and any chance I get to have more sex with him is a bonus in my book. But if he notices you're gone, and asks me if I know where you are, I won't lie for you. I'm sorry, but I can't do that. Not to Asher.'

'That's fair enough. And I wouldn't ask you

to. But you could always change the subject without answering, couldn't you?'

'I'll do what I can.' Her demeanour suddenly changed and she became deadly serious. 'But I won't deceive him. I love him too much to do that. And, I know you don't want to hear this, but what if things don't go to plan with Finlay? I mean, what if tonight is a mistake? If Asher finds out I knew, and kept it from him, he might be furious. I can't jeopardise my relationship with him, Sorcha. I can't. I won't. So please, before you do this, think about it carefully and make sure this is really what you want, and that Finlay is the decent, passionate and adoring man we both believe him to be.'

I took her hands in mine and squeezed them.

'He is, Lottie. I know he is.'

I didn't tell her that I had just discovered he had a secret. A secret big enough to affect the way he lived his life and that he was still paying the price for it today.

But he'd told me it was nothing illegal. And anything that stopped someone getting completely inebriated couldn't be a bad thing, could it?

I wasn't going to let a secret from his past ruin our future.

And besides, I had a few secrets of my own. I hadn't yet told him about my horrendous marriage, for one thing. Not that it was really a secret, I suppose. Everyone in Seahorse Harbour knew about it. Although maybe not all the details.

When Lottie and I returned to our table I could hardly believe my eyes.

Asher was giving Finlay a round of friendly pats on the back, and Mum and Dad were laughing so hard that they looked as if they had tears in their eyes.

'What's going on?' I asked, laughing myself as their merriment was so infectious. Lottie started laughing as well.

'Finlay's been telling us about some of the vehicle insurance claims he's had to deal with,' Dad said, wiping his eyes with the back of his hands while still chuckling away.

Asher shook his head and tried to pull himself together. 'I knew people were inventive, but you won't believe some of the statements his claimants have made. They're hysterical.'

Insurance claims. So Finlay worked for an insurance company. That must have been a reasonably well-paid job. That would have scored him Brownie points with my family, even without him rendering them all hopeless with laughter.

'Can we hear some?' I asked.

Finlay smiled up at me and reached for my hand. I took it and sat down beside him and was amazed to see that none of my family seemed in the least bit bothered by this show of affection.

'Okay,' Finlay said. 'Let me think of some others.' It only took a few seconds. 'Here's one. "A stationary truck was coming the other way when I hit it". Another was "We don't have a Monkey Puzzle Tree, so I realised I had driven into the wrong driveway when I crashed into it" and this one is crazy: "The bus was ten minutes early. It's never early, which was why I collided with it" and a favourite of mine is, "I didn't see the other car in my way when I drove across the central reservation". I don't think people realise what they're writing when they fill out the claim forms.'

'You must have a good memory,' Lottie said, 'to be able to remember those.'

'I have. And the amusing ones stay with you long after you've dealt with the claim. My colleagues and I often compete for a pint in the pub for the funniest excuse for an accident. Although not all accidents are funny. Some are quite the opposite. One or two are unbelievably bad. So it helps to maintain a sense of humour on the job. And speaking of colleagues, I suppose I had better get back to my mates before they send out a search party.' He squeezed my hand as he stood up, smiling at my family. 'It was great to have this opportunity to chat with you all. I hope it's not long before we can do it again.'

'It was lovely to meet you,' Mum said, beaming at him.

'Do you play golf?' Dad asked. 'I'll take you to my golf club. The chaps will love your stories.'

'I do, as it happens. Thanks. I'd love that.' Finlay smiled at him.

'We should get together again before you leave Seahorse Harbour,' Asher said.

'We will,' Finlay replied, before smiling down at me. 'I'll call you this afternoon. Have fun. Bye, everyone.' He gave a little wave and disappeared into the crowd.

'It seems you may have struck gold,' Asher said, once Finlay was out of earshot.

'He's perfect, isn't he?' I enthused.

Finally. After all these years and a stream of disastrous relationships, I had a boyfriend who met with their approval.

And now I knew three more things about him. He had a good job. He had a sense of humour. And he played golf.

But all I kept wondering for most of the afternoon was what Finlay Demon would be like in bed.

And I was counting the hours until I could find out.

Fifteen

Lottie was spending the afternoon with Elsie, and Asher was doing his bit as one of the Seahorse Rider volunteers, working at the small sea life centre called Seahorse Tales.

The Seahorse Riders offices were based in the sea life centre and the volunteers produced newsletters, pamphlets and study notes for kids and adults alike. Kids from nearby schools often went there on organised day trips to learn about the seahorses and other marine life, and in the summer, some of the kids were taken out in boats to get a glimpse of the seahorse's natural habitat – from a safe distance, of course. Children are tactile and would want to pet and play with the little creatures, so it was wise not to let them do that.

The Seahorse Riders also organised fundraising events, sent out letters and leaflets far and wide to bring the plight of seahorses to the attention of the media and the general public, and did a whole lot more. They also took care of injured seahorses, so Asher being a vet came in very handy.

Asher said I could go with him for the afternoon if I wanted.

'Tempting,' I said. 'But when I heard you tell Mum and Dad in the pub that you could only have one drink because you'd be going out in one of the inflatables to check on the seahorses, the offer lost any appeal it might have had, long before you made it.'

'The sea's as calm as a swimming pool today. And I'll make sure you're safe.'

'Still no. Freezing on an inflatable in the English Channel on a February afternoon, might be some people's idea of a good time. But I'm not one of them. Thanks though.'

That wasn't the only reason I didn't want to spend the afternoon with my brother – although it was the main one. The other reason was because, as ridiculous as it was, I was beginning to feel guilty, knowing I was going to be keeping my rendezvous with Finlay a secret from Asher.

'You're welcome to join me and Elsie,' Lottie said.

'That's a much more tempting proposition, but if you don't mind, I'll also say no to that. I want to go for a walk and get some fresh air. Unless you're passionately intent on taking Merry with you, I could take her with me, if you like.'

'It's as cold on land as it is at sea,' Asher said, eyeing me suspiciously. 'Does your sudden urge to go walkabout with Merry have anything to do with the fact that you might bump into Finlay? Because if that's the case, why not simply say so? He seems a decent guy.'

'Praise indeed,' I quipped. 'But that's not the case, actually. I really do want to get some fresh air, and I know for a fact that he'll be with his friends all afternoon.'

'I'm happy for Merry to go for a walk with you,' Lottie said. 'I think she already loves you almost as much as she does me.'

Lottie seemed genuinely pleased about that fact. But then Lottie isn't the type to be resentful or jealous or selfish, I don't think.

'Are you seeing him again?' Asher asked.

'Who, Finlay?' I tried to sound casual. 'Yeah. He's going to call me later to arrange something.'

Asher nodded. 'Mum and Dad liked him, and he doesn't appear to be anything like the other guys you've dated. But try to take things slowly this time, Sorcha. I know you don't want to hear that, and 'slow' isn't in your nature where relationships are concerned.'

'I'll be careful. But as you just said, Finlay isn't like all those other guys. Perhaps my luck has finally changed. Anyway. You'd better get a move on or you'll be late. You said you were meeting Liam at 3, and it's five minutes to right now.'

'Is it? Damn.' He dashed to Lottie and kissed her. 'See you later, sweetheart. Have fun with Elsie.' He turned and waved at me. 'Enjoy your walk. Bye.'

He was out of the door a matter of seconds later and Lottie smiled at me.

'I'm so lucky to have found Asher. I hope you're right about your luck. And I hope you're right about Finlay being The One. You deserve to be as happy as we are.'

I couldn't have agreed with her more.

'Thanks, Lottie. And if you ask me, Asher is the lucky one to have found you. I've honestly never seen him this happy. Even when he qualified as a vet, or when he took over the practice from Barney Short. And believe me, he was ecstatic on both occasions.'

She beamed at me and blushed at the same time.

'That means a lot. Thank you. Now I suppose I'd better love you and leave you. I said I'd be at Mum's at 3, too. If you fancy joining us later feel free to pop round.' She bent down and gave Merry, who was stretched out on her favourite chair near the fire, a big kiss on the head. Merry responded by wagging her tail and licking Lottie's face. 'See you both later then. Bye.'

'Well, that just leaves you and me, kid,' I said to Merry, who wagged her tail harder, jumped down and headed for the 'treat' cupboard in the kitchen.

Naturally, I wouldn't mention this to Lottie, or my brother, because they might tell me I shouldn't do it, but I think the main reason Merry has taken to me so fast is because I often give her treats. I even had to go to TGS – that's The General Store which is at the bottom of Sand Lane and is just set back a bit from Sea Walk, the promenade – to buy some more the other day, so that Lottie and Asher didn't notice that stocks were getting low.

I only gave her one small treat before I put her on her lead and headed outside.

Instinctively, I turned towards the promenade. I really don't know why. The only things down there for Merry to enjoy are the sandy beach, the mass of rocks in the shape of a seahorse's tail, the rock pool, which is deep enough for people to swim in when the tide is out, and the cliffs at each end of the long length of Sea Walk. That runs from the Seahorse Harbour Holiday Park all the way to the sea life centre, Seahorse Tales.

Merry does love the beach. She also loves chasing seagulls and splashing about in the pools on the sand, not just the big rock pool. And she does love swimming. But I didn't fancy dealing with a wet and ultimately smelly dog today, so I decided we'd go somewhere else.

We could've gone to Little Wood, which

really isn't that little. It runs from just across the road from the beach and up behind several of the cottages in Wood Lane and Church Hill, and on for quite some way inland. It also stretches for about a mile, or maybe more, behind Seahorse Harbour Holiday Park. The Holiday Park actually owns part of it but most of it is common land.

You can easily get lost in Little Wood if you don't know your way around. Thankfully, I knew it well. But we'd had some heavy rain a few days ago, and I didn't fancy getting splattered with mud as Merry raced back and forth chasing leaves and squirrels and anything else she could find.

During dry, cold snaps, Little Wood is a magical place. Some of the trees are evergreen and some aren't, so the dappled winter sun casts weird and wonderful shadows on the natural and also the man-made paths. Frost hangs on by its fingers far longer once it takes hold on the branches, and the paths are often covered with a dusting of white sparkling crystals well into the day. The crunch of dead, crisp leaves is often the only sound you can hear as you meander through the towering trees, but sometimes a bird will sing out in the hope that spring will soon be coming.

Today those leaves would still be soggy from the recent downpours, even though yesterday was sunny and windy. At this time of year, it took a long time for the earth in the wood to dry out, so instead I decided to go for a walk over the cliffs.

That meant I couldn't let Merry off her lead in case she chased something, and leapt over the edge of one of them. Lottie told me the first time we met that Merry has a tendency to do that.

But as I'd be taking her down to the beach for her walk that evening, and I'd let her run free down there, I didn't think she'd mind. She wasn't a very demanding dog. Except when it came to treats. And I'd brought that on myself.

We left the cottage in Rope Way and turned onto Church Hill. From there we turned right and walked past the side of The Seahorse Inn, onto Church Row and the shops and cottages there, opposite St Mary Star of the Sea.

Church Row, which was where Asher first saw Lottie, and also where he had proposed, leads directly onto Seahorse Cliffs Road, which is the main road out of the village, and the one I'd be taking to get to Easterhill later. The road travels along the cliff headland for about a mile before turning inland.

The journey to Easterhill takes you past seemingly endless fields which, in the spring, are filled with wild flowers, or frolicking lambs, or cows grazing lazily on fresh shoots of grass.

There's a small dairy farm between

Seahorse Harbour and Easterhill, and that farm also keeps sheep, but many of the other fields grow arable crops of wheat, oats and barley, and rape is used as a 'break crop' on those.

I can still remember the first time we came to Seahorse Harbour via the road from Easterhill. It was in August and my eyes couldn't get enough of the staggered blocks of golden corn, bright yellow rape, deep red poppies, and soft blues, pinks, purples and whites of wildflowers or the green fields dotted with sheep and cows. The sky was a vivid, cloudless blue and birds flitted overhead, singing to one another.

'Is this paradise?' I asked Mum and Dad.

'Yes, baby girl,' Dad said. 'I believe it is.'

We certainly had a wonderful holiday, so much so that we often came back. Although not as often as some.

I heard Lilith Shoe call my name just before Merry and I reached the driveway to Mikkel Meloy's grand house, which is set back from the road and perched on the cliff overlooking the bay and Seahorse Point.

Seahorse Point is where you'll find The Weeping Eye, which really does look like an eye. The edges and sides of the circular hole in the cliff look like an iris, and there's a cave below, containing a pool, which during the summer is a shimmering blue.

When the tide comes in, the sea rushes into the cave and shoots up through the circular hole, as a spout of water. Which is why it's called The Weeping Eye. If you stand too close, when the tide comes in, you'll get soaked.

You can climb down into the cave, but it's not advisable. You can also swim into it via the inlet leading to The Shallows, but again, you shouldn't. There's a fierce Rip Current and when the tide comes in, it can be lethal. Asher and the rest of The Seahorse Riders know the waters well, but even they have to be careful. Several people have lost their lives due to that current and the rocks at the foot of Seahorse Point. People still jump off Seahorse Point into the sea below, as a dare. Some don't live to tell the tale.

'Coo-ey!' Lilith waved in a demented fashion, like one of those inflatable tube-shaped men that bounce to and fro with long flapping arms that you sometimes see outside shops. 'Sorcha!'

She hurried across the road without looking, but there isn't usually a lot of traffic on that road.

'Hello, Lilith,' I said. 'It's bitterly cold today, isn't it? Not really a day for standing around and chatting.'

I hoped she'd take the hint.

She didn't.

'Who was that handsome young man I saw

you with at Asher and Lottie's engagement party? I do hope you've finally found someone nice. I couldn't believe it when I heard what that last one, Sean did. And you hadn't been dating long, had you?' She tutted loudly. 'I don't understand men these days. So what's this Finlay like?'

She knew his name, but then she was at the engagement party so she probably heard it there. Knowing Lilith, she probably already knew more about him than I did.

'He's lovely.'

'Such a pity he's leaving on Tuesday. Not really enough time to get to know him well. Although you can know a person their entire life and never really know them. Now I'm not one to gossip, as you know, but only last week I heard that Beryl Tavington discovered her late husband had another wife and family! It all came out when she read his will. It was one of those homemade wills and he'd written down all the details because he wanted Beryl to split everything with the other woman. Well, he was dead, so he couldn't go to prison for bigamy, could he? But it just goes to show you. And only yesterday I was told that Prue Lazenby is expecting. That's Agatha Lazenby's granddaughter. She's only sixteen and she doesn't even have a boyfriend.' Lilith leaned closer. 'One of those one-night hook ups, or whatever it is they're called. What is it with young people and sex these days? They can never seem to get enough of it. In my day, we weren't like that.'

I didn't know Beryl Tavington, or Agatha and Prue Lazenby, but I don't suppose they'd be thrilled to know that Lilith was telling everyone about their situations.

'Gosh, it really is cold. Please don't let me keep you.'

'You're not, dear. It was wonderful to see Asher so happy at the party. He and Lottie make such a delightful couple. What a good thing Josie picked Liam over Asher, or things might've been very different. But Fate has a way of sorting things out, don't you think?'

I didn't like her gossiping about Asher, but I did agree with her about Destiny, as I prefer to call it. Fate always sounds as if it's something bad. Destiny, on the other hand, sounds good.

'I do. I firmly believe in Destiny.'

She nodded sagely. 'I thought you and Nathan Bromley might make a go of it.'

'What?'

I couldn't believe my ears.

'You and Nathan Bromley, dear. But then he's not the type of man you fall for, is he? You prefer the bad boys. Nathan's not like that. That man has a heart of gold. What he's given up just to come here and help Lyn proves that.'

I was going to say that I didn't prefer bad boys but I was so intrigued by her comment about what Nathan had given up that I let that comment slide.

'Oh? What's he given up then?'

She looked genuinely shocked.

'Don't you know? I thought you did. Well, I'm not one to gossip, but this isn't really gossip, is it? He was offered a partnership in that posh firm of architects he worked for. He came down to spend a weekend with Lyn and just one week later, he turned up on her doorstep telling her he'd jacked it in and wanted to help her in the café instead. She thought it had all got too much for him and that he needed some time to unwind. But then she heard him take a call one day and that's when she discovered the truth. The firm had called with an offer to double his share, by making him an equity partner instead of a salaried partner if he'd go back, but he told them his family needed him and he had to put them first. Lyn had it out with him and he admitted that he'd seen she was struggling to cope and decided he wanted to help. When she said he was throwing away his future, he brushed it off and said he had other plans so it was no big deal.'

'I didn't even know he was an architect.'

It was true. I didn't. But it was a silly thing to say after what I'd just heard. Had Nathan really given up a dazzling future to help his aunt? And did he really have other plans? He'd said something similar to me the other night. Although he hadn't mentioned the bit about giving everything up to help Lyn.

What an incredibly selfless thing to do. Not many people would do that. I'm not sure I would. To leave a fantastic job and come and work in a little café, to keep someone else's dream alive was the sort of thing that made a man a bit of a hero in my eyes.

Perhaps I'd misjudged Nathan Bromley.

Perhaps there was more to him than I thought.

But he still wasn't Finlay Demon.

Just the thought of Finlay made me tingle all over.

The thought of Nathan made me ... cross.

Sixteen

'Now you know that Asher likes Finlay,' Lottie said that evening when she and I were in the kitchen making supper, 'maybe you don't have to sneak out tonight. Maybe you could just say you're going to meet Finlay, and Asher will be fine about it.'

She had a point. Surely as a fit, healthy, red-blooded male, Asher would understand. I know for a fact that he and Lottie had sex very soon after they met because Lottie told me so. She also added that it was the best sex she'd ever had, which was a bit too much information for me to tell you the truth.

But what a man might do in certain circumstances, and what he'd be happy for a man to do with his sister, are two completely different things. And Asher has always been very protective of me, I decided against telling him. Especially as Finlay had called me in the afternoon to say we would have to meet much later than planned.

'I can't get away before 11 tonight. I'm really sorry, but my mates have booked a Ghost Walk and a dinner in a haunted house in Easterhill and I honestly can't get out of it. They'll be livid if I try because Andy has booked this especially for me. He knows I'm into ghosts and stuff. At least I'll be able to go straight to the hotel afterwards. And we'll have the entire night together.'

I struggled to hide my disappointment, but at least I now knew something else about him. He liked ghosts and spooky stuff. I wasn't sure how I felt about that. Scary films make me run for cover.

'That's a pity,' I said. 'Or not, I suppose, as you like that stuff. But it's okay. We'll have the night together as you say. I'll meet you at the hotel around 11 then.'

'Great. Thanks for being so understanding. I'll make it up to you, I promise.'

If I told Asher that I was off to meet Finlay at that time of night, he'd think it was just to have sex, and as much as Asher liked Finlay, I was pretty sure he wouldn't approve.

Nathan Bromley definitely wouldn't.

Not that I cared what that man thought.

After hearing what Nathan had done for his aunt, I wondered if I'd been unfair towards him. He soon showed me I hadn't.

I saw him again when I took Merry for her walk. I'd gone down to the beach as I'd planned earlier but I walked along the promenade towards the café instead of simply heading straight onto the sand. I had no idea why I'd done that. It was almost as if I wanted to bump into the man. Which of course I didn't.

And how was I supposed to know he'd be at Seahorse Bites Café at 10 p.m. on a Sunday night? The café closes at 6.30 on Sundays.

I think I had heard Lyn mention at some time or other that her darling nephew did the weekly accounts on Sunday night, but I didn't know he did them at the café.

I saw the lights were on as soon as I stepped onto the promenade and as I got closer, I saw Nathan seated at a table in the window to the other side of the glass front door. I spotted the sign on the door saying 'CLOSED' beneath which hung the large sign and a picture of a scruffy-looking dog stating, 'Dogs welcome, along with well-behaved humans.' That sign always made me smile.

I hadn't realised I was standing still and staring inside until Nathan ran a hand through his hair and suddenly looked up. It was as if he could sense my presence.

He seemed as surprised as I was but a smile flashed across his face and he jumped up and hurried towards the door.

I cursed under my breath and quickly turned away.

'Sorcha!' His tone was a mixture of

something between happy and desperate.

I took a deep breath and swivelled round to face him, bending down to let Merry off her lead at the same time.

'I didn't expect to see you down here at this time of night.'

He grinned. 'I was here this time, and later, last night. You waved and yelled at me as you, Lottie and Asher left Elsie's.'

'Last night? I don't remember that. Are you sure it was me?'

'Yes. And I just said you were with Asher and Lottie. But you were clearly rather drunk.'

'Whatever. I don't remember seeing you.'

'And I was here at this time, and later, on Friday night too. You do remember seeing me on Friday, don't you?'

'Of course I do. But don't you have anything better to do than spend every night here?'

He gave a little laugh and scratched his head. 'Sadly, no.'

I was surprised by his honesty. Not that I'm saying I expected him to lie because I didn't. Somehow I couldn't imagine Nathan telling a lie. Except he had lied to Lyn.

I don't know why I said it, and I certainly hadn't intended to, but the words tumbled out before I could stop them.

'I didn't know you were an architect. I hear you gave up the opportunity to become a partner, just so that you could give Lyn a hand. That was very noble of you.'

I'm not sure if he was more surprised than cross, or more cross than surprised.

'It wasn't noble at all. Lyn's my aunt and she needed my help. It was as simple as that. Anyone would've done what I did.'

'They wouldn't. I'm sure I wouldn't. Especially not if I had the chance to double my income by becoming an equity partner in a posh firm.'

'Who told you that? Lilith Shoe, if I hazard a guess. But I can't imagine how she found out. I'm sure Lyn wouldn't have told her.'

'You know Lilith. You can't keep secrets from her.'

'It wasn't a secret, exactly. It's just none of anyone else's business.'

'You would've had a fantastic lifestyle, Nathan. How could you give all that up to come here?'

'I suppose that depends on what you see as "a fantastic lifestyle". Working all hours of the day and night in an air-conditioned office, meeting deadlines and targets, or being able to breathe in fresh air and see the sea every day, while helping someone you love, at the same time.'

'I'm not sure there's much fresh air in the kitchen of the café.' I laughed. 'But helping someone you love is rewarding, I suppose.

Even if you did have to lie to them to do it.'

'I didn't lie. I merely withheld the truth.'

'Isn't that the same thing?'

'No. I don't think so.'

'So you think it's okay to withhold the truth?'

'In certain circumstances, yes. I knew Lyn would be upset at the thought of me giving up what, like you, she saw as a bright future. If I had told her what I was going to do, she would've tried to stop me. Once I'd made up my mind to do it, there was little point in telling her something that would only have made her feel guilty when she had no reason to be. It was my choice and it's my life. I only did what felt right to me.'

His words had far more impact than he could've imagined. That was almost exactly how I felt about me going to spend the night with Finlay. I'd told Lottie that I wasn't lying to Asher, I was simply withholding the truth by not telling him what I had planned.

'I totally agree with you about that. It's not really a lie, especially if it's done for all the best reasons.'

He was giving me a strange look.

'Why do I get the feeling that we're no longer talking about my situation? Is there something you're trying to tell me?'

'What? No. Nothing.'

The look intensified and I suddenly felt like

a naughty schoolgirl standing in front of a wiser adult.

'Sorcha. I am a friend, you know. If something is worrying you, or there's something you want to talk about, you can talk to me. I promise whatever you say will stay between us.'

I tried to make a joke of it. 'Lilith Shoe will still find out.'

'Not from me.'

I don't know why I told him, but somehow, he looked so approachable, so understanding. Caring, even.

'I'm going to do something tonight and I haven't told Asher. It's nothing bad, and it's none of anyone's business, but I know that if I told him, he would probably try and stop me. So I'm not going to tell him. But it sort of feels as though I'm lying to him. Except I'm not. I'm simply withholding the truth. Like you did.'

His entire body seemed to tense in front of my eyes. The caring look disappeared from his, and his jaw clenched as he lifted his head slightly in an almost confrontational gesture.

'This wouldn't have anything to do with Finlay Demon, would it?'

Even his voice was suddenly cold.

'Yes.' I sounded as timid as a mouse.

'Dear God, Sorcha. Please tell me you are not going to spend the night with him.'

'Er. I am. I'm meeting him at the Easterhill

Hotel and Spa. He's booked a room.'

'You don't know a thing about him. Don't do this, Sorcha. You don't have to, you know. You can say no.'

'You make it sound as though he's forcing me.'

'Not forcing. Persuading. Convincing you it's what you want to do.'

I laughed and shook my head. 'I didn't need any convincing or persuading. Believe me, Nathan, it is what I want to do. In fact, I can't wait.'

He took a step back, almost as if I had slapped him.

'You're unbelievable. Are you insane? You've only just got out of another failed relationship. Are you really going to jump straight into yet another?'

My mouth gaped open and I blinked in astonishment, but it wasn't long before I pulled myself together.

'Thanks for the support. So much for being a friend. Clearly there are some things I can't tell you.'

'Clearly there are. What did you expect me to say? That you were doing the right thing by not telling Asher? Creeping around behind his back isn't very sensible. And why would you want to do that anyway? He'll be hurt when he finds out.'

'No he won't. He'll understand. He slept

with Lottie shortly after they met. And I'm not creeping around. Finlay and I are just doing what two people in love always do.'

'Two people in love? You only met the guy on Friday night.'

'So what? You've heard of love at first sight. You may not have experienced it. In fact, I'm pretty sure you haven't. I'm not even sure you've ever been in love, have you? I've never seen you with a girlfriend.'

'I've had girlfriends and yes, I've been in love. But I'll tell you one thing I haven't done, and never would. I've never asked anyone to creep around behind their family's back and meet me at some hotel just to have sex.'

'He didn't ask me to. And I've already said we're not creeping around. And it's not "just to have sex". We're in love.'

'I'm sure you think you are, but what about him? Has he told you he's in love with you?'

'Yes, he has. Why does that surprise you? Don't you think a man could possibly fall in love with me? Just because I've had several bad relationships in the past, it doesn't mean I'd never find a man who loves me. I have found one. And it's Finlay Demon.'

'Plenty of men could fall in love with you, Sorcha. I have no doubt of that. Believe me. But if he's so in love with you, and he believes you're in love with him, why isn't he shouting it from the rooftops? If you told me you loved me,

I know I would be.'

'You would? Wow. That's a surprise. I can't imagine you being that romantic. But then again, I can't imagine you being in love with anyone. And for your information, the reason neither of us is shouting anything from the rooftops just yet, is because I know what everyone would say. They'd say, "Sorcha's fallen in love yet again. Let's see how long this one lasts." And I don't want to hear that. Because this time it's going to last.'

He was shaking his head as though he thought he was wasting his breath talking to me.

'Oh God, Sorcha. Why can't you see...?' He cleared his throat and looked me directly in the eye. 'For your sake, I hope you're right. I hope this guy is everything you think he is, and more. I hope you've found what you're looking for, and that he makes you happy. I am a friend, even though I might not seem so, sometimes. But remember this, I'm here if you need me.'

'Need you? Why would I need you? Sorry. I didn't mean it like that. But you've basically just told me that you don't think Finlay really loves me, and now you're saying I might need you, as if I might want a shoulder to cry on or something. Well thanks, but I won't. This time it's different. He's different. I'm sure of it. And I must go because I've got to get ... Oh my God.' I spun round and scanned the beach. 'Where's

Merry. I'd completely forgotten about her.'

'Me too. But I can see her. She's there on the rocks, in that shaft of moonlight. But I think she…'

His voice trailed off and he was running down the beach before I even realised what was happening.

Seventeen

'She's bleeding!' I yelped, barking instructions at Nathan. 'Put her down gently. Get a cloth. We need to get her warm and dry before she freezes to death. Where are you going?'

She wasn't the only one who needed to get dry, I suddenly realised. Nathan was soaked to the skin, having jumped into the massive rock pool to get Merry out after she'd lost her footing on the rocks and tumbled in. The pool was wonderfully warm to swim in during the summer when the sun warmed the waters to almost swimming pool temperatures, but at this time of year, it would've been bitterly cold. I could almost see Nathan shivering. Merry definitely was as she lay huddled in Nathan's arms.

'I'm taking her home. You're right. She does need to get warm and dry. She also needs a vet. Are you coming?'

He'd already raced past me but he shot a quick glance back over his shoulder.

I was so shocked that I hadn't moved, but now I ran after them and caught up, still jogging to keep pace as Nathan headed towards Asher's.

Thankfully, my brother's cottage is just a couple of minutes from the beach, and when we got close, I ran ahead and opened the door. Nathan hesitated for a nano-second as if he were unsure whether he should bring Merry to the front door of the cottage or take her to the side door which was the entrance to the veterinary practice.

I might've laughed if I hadn't been so worried that I'd almost killed Lottie's beloved dog.

'There's a door to the surgery from in here,' I said. 'The street door to the surgery's locked.'

'Of course.' He followed me inside.

'Asher! Asher we need you. Merry fell into the rock pool and I think she may be hurt. She's freezing too. Asher!'

'I'm coming!'

He appeared a moment or two later, still dressing as he reached the top of the stairs. Lottie was right behind him, and all she was wearing was a dressing gown.

'Merry! Merry, my darling. Are you okay?'

To my astonishment, Merry gave a little bark as if to set Lottie's mind at ease. But it was a pretty pitiful bark so it had the opposite effect, especially on me.

'Oh my God! You've got to save her, Asher. You've got to. This is all my fault! I'm so, so sorry. What can I do to help?'

'You can stop shrieking, for a start,' Asher said, 'and give me some room so that I can take a look at her.' He shot a look at Lottie and squeezed her arm. 'Try not to panic. I'm sure she'll be okay. I can already see the cut and it doesn't look too deep.' He nodded a sort of 'Thank you,' to Nathan as he turned towards his surgery. 'Bring her in here, please.'

Nathan gently placed Merry on the table in the surgery and Asher gave her a thorough but fast once over.

'Grab a towel from in there, please Nathan.' He indicated the store room to his left. 'Any one will do. They're all clean.'

He carefully lifted Merry and carried her to the large stainless-steel sink where he held her with one hand while turning on the spray tap to the finest setting and softly washing away the salt water and fragments of seaweed that had caught in her sodden fur. Nathan held the towel until Asher was ready and as Asher dried her, Nathan stroked her head and whispered words of encouragement and praise.

'You'll be fine,' he said. 'You're such a good girl. And you know you're in the best hands possible.'

Anyone would've thought it was his dog, but as I hugged Lottie and held her hand, I could see her smiling at Nathan, Asher and of course, her beloved dog.

'She will be, won't she?' Lottie asked, sounding more confident than I still felt.

Asher nodded and smiled, relief written all over his face.

'She'll be as good as new. As I thought, the cut isn't deep but it will need a couple of stitches. She'll need plenty of rest, some fluids, and lots of cuddles. All of which she'll have. By tomorrow, she'll probably have forgotten all about this.'

'I won't,' I said. 'I really am sorry. I should've been taking better care of her.'

'Don't blame yourself,' Lottie said, now the one doing the comforting. 'She's always getting herself into scrapes. At least it was just the rocks she fell off, not the cliffs. And if Asher says she's fine, I know she is, so the panic is over.' She beamed at Nathan. 'Thank you for saving her. I can see you did because you're saturated. Asher? Do you have something Nathan can change into? He needs a hot shower or he'll be the one catching pneumonia.'

'Jesus, yes. Take him upstairs, Sorcha. You know where my clothes are. Nathan, you're welcome to anything. Take your pick. There's plenty of hot water and Sorcha will show you the shower.'

'I'll be fine. I can shower at Lyn's.'

'Don't be ridiculous,' I said. 'Apart from the fact you're dripping all over the floor, it's freezing out and even walking the few minutes home is several minutes too far. Come with me.'

Lottie took Nathan's place beside Merry and after smiling sheepishly at her and Asher, he followed me back into the cottage and up the stairs, although he did stop in the kitchen to take his shoes, socks, coat and jumper off first, which was rather thoughtful of him. There was already a trail of sand and salt water leading from the front door to the surgery and although he was still dripping, it was nowhere near as much.

'The shower's there,' I said, pointing to the bathroom. 'I'll get you a towel and I'll find you some clothes for when you get out.'

'Thanks,' he said.

'I'm the one who should be thanking you. I'm not sure what I would've done if you hadn't been there. Although if you hadn't been there, we wouldn't have been arguing and I would've taken better care of Merry, so she wouldn't have been on the rocks in the first place.'

He grinned. 'I had a feeling this might end up being my fault. And I am sorry we argued. Which reminds me.' The grin vanished. 'Don't you have a *rendezvous* to keep?'

'Oh God! Yes. I'd totally forgotten. I'm astonished you reminded me. I thought you didn't think I should go.'

'I didn't and I still don't. But I want you to be happy. And besides, you'd no doubt blame me for making you miss it.'

I grinned at him. 'You're probably right. But I'm not sure I should go, after what's happened. I want to, obviously. I *really* want to.'

'Yes. Thanks. I don't need reminding of that fact.'

'Okay. Don't get cross again. Go and take your shower.' I shoved him into the bathroom. 'I'll be back in a second with your towel.'

I don't know how he managed to remove his clothes so fast as I really was only a second or two getting him a towel. The airing cupboard was merely a few steps away. I suppose, on reflection, I should've grabbed a towel before I shoved him into the bathroom. But then again if I had, I wouldn't have got to see him naked. And as much as I hate to admit it, Nathan Bromley, naked, is a pretty impressive sight.

I thought he would be embarrassed, like he was in the café that day he was wearing his aunt's yellow apron and Josie had made those suggestive comments. I know I would've died on the spot if our roles had been reversed. But after an initial look of surprise, he simply reached out his hand for the towel I was holding, clearing his throat and raising his brows when I didn't immediately pass it over.

'Sorry,' I said, managing to drag my admiring gaze to his face.

He took the towel and grinned.

'No problem. But from the expression on your face, anyone would think you've never seen a naked man before. And we both know that's not true.'

'I've never seen *you* naked before,' I said, slightly disappointed that the towel was now obscuring my view, although as he held it casually in front of him, I thought it might move at any moment and allow me to see more.

'When you've seen one, you've seen us all. Unlike women, there's not really a great deal of difference between us men.'

'I can't believe you said that. Just like us, no two men are the same.'

He shrugged. 'I'll take your word for that. I don't take much notice of other men's physiques.' He grinned again. 'I'm obviously not as interested in them as you seem to be.' He coughed once more. 'Sorcha? Are you going to stand there and watch me take a shower? I don't mind at all. You can even come and join me if you like.'

'What? God no! Oh! Er. Sorry. I didn't mean to stare. I...'

Now I was utterly and completely embarrassed. I'd been ogling him and enjoying it and he damn well knew it.

And when I still didn't move, he gave me

another good look by removing the towel and slowly hanging it over the heated towel rail.

I sort of choked and spluttered and in my hurry to turn away and run out of the room, I bashed my head against the door.

The impact sent me backwards a step and I immediately felt his hands on my arms, and his body against mine, steadying me, although he did move slightly away, so that just his hands held me upright.

'Jesus! Are you okay?'

I could hear the concern in his voice but I couldn't turn to look at him. I was well aware that he was starkers and was standing right behind me.

All sorts of images flashed before my eyes, like a movie on fast forward, and as most of them involved me and Nathan doing things I'd been dreaming of doing with Finlay, I was sure I was suffering from concussion.

'I'm fine,' I lied. 'Er. I just need to go and sit down. My head's spinning.'

'I bet it is. I'll help you to your room. Which one is it?'

'No, you won't!'

I didn't mean to shriek, but honestly. Was the man completely insane?

Didn't he know what might happen if he took me to my room and laid me down on my bed? Hadn't he seen any romantic movies? The guy was naked, for goodness sake. And I'd made it clear that I liked what I'd seen.

Or was I the only one of us who was thinking along those lines?

Didn't it occur to him that he'd be in my bedroom, naked, laying me on my bed as I stared up into his eyes? How did he imagine that scene might play out?

Or wasn't he imagining anything about us at all? Wasn't he even the slightest bit turned on by this? Didn't he think, for just one second, that he could slide his hand from my arm to my breast? Or that he could press himself against me again and trail kisses down my neck? Or turn me around and kiss me passionately on the lips?

Didn't he want to do any of those things?

Didn't he find me in the least bit attractive?

'Sorcha?' His voice was hoarse and little more than a whisper. 'I don't want you to take this the wrong way, but if you're sure you're okay to walk, I'm afraid I need you to get out of here, please.'

'I'm fine,' I managed. 'And I'll go, don't worry.'

He let go of me before I'd finished speaking.

'Right now, if possible.'

Bloody cheek! Was he that desperate to have his shower?

I pushed my shoulders back and marched out, being careful not to collide with the door this time, which I slammed shut behind me, in a somewhat childish tantrum.

And when he appeared in the open doorway of my room about ten or so minutes later, thankfully with the towel wrapped tightly around his waist, to ask if I'd found something for him to wear, I was still so annoyed with him that I shouted, 'Oh for God's sake, Nathan. They're on the bed next door. Now bloody well leave me alone!'

This time he was the one who closed the door. Although he didn't slam it.

Eighteen

I'd missed three calls from Finlay by the time I remembered I was supposed to be meeting him. Nathan had reminded me, but after what happened in the bathroom, the only man occupying my thoughts was Nathan bloody Bromley, himself.

And I really wasn't happy about that at all.

How could this be possible?

How could this have happened?

It must have been delayed shock after Merry's accident. That was the only thing that made any sense.

The only explanation.

Because there was no way on this earth that I could have suddenly discovered that I might very well be in love with Nathan sodding Bromley.

No way.

Nah-uh.

Not on your nelly.

Not on anyone's nelly.

Not if he were the only man left on the planet.

I. Could. Not. Be. In Love. With. That bloody man.

Destiny wouldn't be that cruel to me.

She wouldn't.

For the first time in my life I'd met a decent man called Finlay Demon.

A man who loved me at first sight and who was waiting for me in a hotel room so that we could show one another how we felt.

But now the only man I wanted to show how I felt was the one man I disliked the most.

Okay. That wasn't true. I didn't dislike Nathan. But I did find him irritating.

I certainly didn't find him attractive.

Until now.

It was definitely the knock on my head that had caused this, when the door jumped out and hit me.

For a moment I laughed.

That sounded like one of those insurance claims Finlay had told us about in the pub.

'It wasn't my fault,' I'd say, if anyone asked. 'The door jumped out and hit me and made me think I had fallen in love with someone I would never have fallen in love with under any other circumstances.'

Except I'd been staring dreamily at Nathan's wonderful body long before the door hit me.

And the saying is, 'You need to have some sense bashed into you', not 'You need to have the sense bashed out of you'. On that basis, it would mean that I was being stupid before and that the bashing had brought me to my senses.

But that meant it was Nathan I was really in love with, not Finlay.

That couldn't be the case.

I really didn't want to be in love with Nathan Bromley.

Although would that be such a bad thing?

Yes, of course it would. Because if I was in love with Nathan it would mean that yet again, I'd fallen for a man who didn't feel the same way about me.

I was pretty sure that I was the last woman Nathan would ever fall in love with, despite his teasing about joining him in the shower. That had just been a joke between friends.

And that was one of the problems. Nathan and I were friends. Not very good friends. Not even close friends, but we were still friends, in spite of the fact that I'd told Finlay we weren't. And other people too.

It was as if I didn't want to be friends with Nathan. As if I didn't want to admit I had any feelings for him at all.

Until now.

And I was pretty sure that Nathan just saw me as a friend, and that he'd never see me as anything else.

What I needed was a good night's sleep.

I'd probably laugh about all this in the morning.

But before I went to bed, I had to return Finlay's calls and break the news that I wouldn't be joining him that night.

I told him about Merry's accident – but not about Nathan's involvement. I merely said that a friend who happened to be nearby, saved her and took her to Asher with me.

I did tell Finlay about hitting my head on a door, but again, not the part Nathan played in that.

And then I said, 'I'm truly sorry, Finlay, but all things considered, would you mind if I didn't meet you at the hotel tonight? I've got a splitting headache, so I don't think I'd be much fun. I'll go halves with you on the cost.'

He was silent for a second or two and I thought he might be angry. But he wasn't.

'Don't worry about it. If I hadn't cancelled on you earlier, we wouldn't be in this situation now. I could do with a good night's sleep in a comfy bed and without snoring mates. The beds in the Holiday Park are fine, but they're nothing to write home about. I might even have a treatment in the spa. It's open until 2 a.m., if you can believe that. I'll call you in the morning and we can do something then. Sweet dreams, Sorcha. I know who I'll be dreaming about.'

'Same here,' I said.

There was absolutely no point in telling him who I'd probably be dreaming about – because I had a feeling it wouldn't be him.

I just hoped that when I awoke, I'd be back to normal. And that I'd find I was in love with Finlay and not an entirely different man, called Nathan bloody Bromley.

Nineteen

The next morning, I opened my eyes to sunshine streaming through my bedroom window and despite the fact that I had woken up a couple of times during the night after some confusing dreams, I had a feeling it was going to be a very good day.

That feeling was confirmed when I went downstairs for breakfast and saw Merry wagging her tail and munching her food as if she had indeed forgotten the entire drama of yesterday evening, just as Asher said she would.

'How is she?' I asked, bending down to stroke her head.

'Even better than I expected,' Asher said. 'Although she doesn't like the plastic cone I tried to put on her this morning to prevent her from biting at her stitches. I'll try a different type once she's had breakfast.'

'I'm so relieved she's okay. I'm really sorry it happened. If I'm ever allowed to take her out again, I promise I'll take much better care of her.'

Lottie joined us in the kitchen, having clearly just got out of the shower. She was towel drying her hair and only wore her dressing gown.

'Of course you'll be allowed to take her out,' she said, smiling sympathetically. 'I told you last night that she's always getting into scrapes. We don't blame you. Once she's off the lead, she can disappear within seconds. And it was dark on the beach.'

'Yes. But that's the point. I should've kept my eyes on her the entire time instead of arguing with ... with Nathan.'

I hadn't meant to disclose that. But I realised I'd gone too far and couldn't get out of it.

'Arguing with Nathan?' There was a troubled look on Asher's face. 'Why were you arguing with Nathan?'

I dropped onto a chair and leant my elbows on the kitchen table.

'Oh I don't know. I always seem to end up arguing with the man. He can be extremely annoying.'

Asher grinned. 'Says the pot calling the kettle black.'

I pulled a face at him. 'Funny.'

'Is that why he seemed to be in such a strange mood when he left?' Lottie queried.

'He did seem a bit odd,' Asher confirmed. 'I asked if he wanted to stay for a beer, and he mumbled something about not wanting to be in the way. I told him he wasn't, and that a beer was the least we owed him for saving Merry. He replied that we owed him nothing, and that he'd return my clothes today. And then he was gone. I thought he was probably just cold and tired. But maybe there was more to it than that. Surely you can remember what you argued about, Sorcha?'

'I can't. Relationships, I think. He told me, in a roundabout way that he doesn't approve of my choices.'

Asher laughed. 'You can't hang the man for that. Few people approve of your choices. Usually. Although your recent choice appears to be a great improvement.'

'Finlay, you mean?'

'Is there someone else I should know about?'

'No one. Absolutely no one.'

'Are you seeing him today?' Lottie asked tentatively.

'Nathan?'

'No. Finlay.'

Asher laughed again. 'You seem to have Nathan on the brain.'

'No I don't. I absolutely *do not*. And yes, I'm seeing Finlay. He's going to call me this morning.'

'You didn't go out again last night?' Lottie asked, flicking a guilty look at Asher then back at me.

'No. I went to bed.'

'Why did you think she might've gone out again?'

Lottie shook her head. 'No reason. I thought I heard the door, but I was obviously wrong.'

'I didn't. Honestly I didn't.'

'It's okay, Sorcha,' Asher said. 'There's no need to be so defensive. You can come and go as you please. You know that.'

I met Lottie's eyes and shook my head. She clearly thought I had gone to Easterhill as planned, and I wanted her to know that I hadn't, and that I wasn't lying.

She smiled and nodded as if she understood. 'It was probably a dream or something. Dreams can seem very real, can't they?'

'Tell me about it.'

She was right about that. My dreams had seemed incredibly real last night and I didn't know if I was pleased or sad when I woke in the very early hours to discover that my dream about making love with Nathan was exactly that – a dream.

And yet I woke up feeling cheerful and optimistic.

Perhaps I was right. All I needed was some

sleep to put my feelings for Nathan in perspective. He was a friend, and that was all he would be.

Finlay Demon was my future.

Asher glanced at his watch. 'I'd better get a move on. I've got an appointment with a beagle called Bertie, at 9 and I need to get some paperwork done before that.' He kissed Lottie on the lips, ruffled Merry's furry head, and did the same to my hair.

'Get off,' I said, laughing as I pushed him away.

'I'll nip back in to try another cone before I see Bertie,' he said.

'I'm sorry I nearly dropped you in it,' Lottie said, once Asher had closed the door leading to the surgery. 'I don't know what I was thinking.'

I grinned at her. 'No harm done. I called him and cancelled. He took it really well and I'm hoping we can rearrange something for today.'

'You're still going ahead with it then?'

'Absolutely. The first chance I get. Why? Don't you think I should?'

She shrugged. 'I'm not sure now. I know Asher and I had sex within a couple of days of our very first meeting, but it happened naturally. It wasn't planned. I was thinking about that during the evening before I suggested our early night.'

'Which I asked you to do and then I

promptly ruined it.'

'No, you didn't.' She grinned at me. 'Well, not much.' She knelt on the floor beside Merry and lovingly petted her. 'But I was thinking that it might not be as good if it's planned. Doesn't it take all the romance out of it?'

'Some of it, I suppose. But it makes it exciting. The anticipation yesterday was incredible. Until Nathan spoiled it. And I felt so guilty about Merry and so cross with Nathan that all the wind went out of my sails.'

'So you cancelled?'

'Yes!'

'Don't shout at me, but doesn't that tell you something?'

I stared at her for a few seconds and I heard the kitchen clock ticking on the wall.

'I'm afraid it doesn't. You'll have to enlighten me.'

'You're cross.'

I shook my head. 'I'm not. I genuinely have no idea what you're saying.'

She sucked in a breath and cleared her throat as she let it out.

'I'm saying that I want to make love with Asher all the time. Every minute of the day and night. We don't, of course, but I think about him constantly. He's the person I want to be with if I'm not feeling great, or if something happens, or ... what I'm trying to say is, that if I were in your shoes last night, and I knew

Asher was waiting for me in a hotel room, nothing would've stopped me from going to him, not even Merry's accident. I'd want to be with the man I loved. But that's just me. That's what I would've done if I were you.'

She stood up and went to the kettle, switching it on before turning back to me.

I sat in silence and watched her, mulling over what she'd said. I nodded when she took two cups from the cupboard and held one up, using the gesture to ask if I wanted coffee.

'So what you're suggesting is that I might not be as in love with Finlay as I claim to be? Because if I was, I'd have wanted to go and be with him after what happened.'

She shrugged. 'I'm only saying that I would've gone. But we're two completely different people. Although in some ways I think we're very similar. We both want to be loved by one special person and to spend our lives with that man.'

'Isn't that what most people want?'

'Maybe. But lots of people want careers too. Or other things. I don't think I've ever really wanted that. And neither have you.'

'You're right. All I want is to find my Prince Charming. And I thought I finally had.'

'Finlay?'

'Yes. But now I'm beginning to wonder.'

'Because of what I just said? I hope I haven't caused a problem.'

'You haven't. And it isn't just because of what you said.'

I sighed deeply and shook my head as I ran my hands through my hair, which was still tangled from sleep because I hadn't had a shower yet.

'Has something else made you have doubts?'

I met her questioning gaze and nodded slowly.

'I think so, yes. Or no. I don't know.'

'Would you like to talk about it?'

'No. He's the last person I want to talk about.'

'He? Finlay you mean?' Lottie looked as confused as I felt.

'No. Nathan Bromley.'

But in spite of saying I didn't want to talk about him I found myself telling Lottie every single detail of what had happened between Nathan and me last night.

Twenty

Later that day, soon after lunch, as Lottie and I took Merry for a walk – this time through Little Wood, with Merry on a short lead so that she couldn't race into something and cause problems with her stitches, the subject of Nathan came up again.

Possibly because I couldn't stop thinking about the man and I didn't know what to do about that.

The problem was, we'd met Diana and Josie, who had come for a walk with Diana's dog Henry to discuss issues of their own.

Diana told us on Saturday at Elsie's that she and Alex had made up after the drama at the engagement party, but now she said that for some reason, she was finding this latest piece of information about her husband's string of affairs, more difficult to come to terms with than she'd thought.

'It's stupid, I realise that,' she said. 'It was years ago and I know about the affairs he's had since, but the fact that he forgot her, just simply forgot her, as if she meant less than nothing to him, has made me feel a little differently. I can't really explain it. I'm still crazy about him and I'm sure that'll never change, but something definitely has.'

'Are you regretting your decision to take him back?' Josie asked, clearly surprised by the news.

'No. I don't think so. But I think I've lost some of my respect for him.' She laughed mirthlessly. 'I know that sounds crazy and you're all wondering how I can possibly respect a man who has cheated on me so many times, with so many women, but he's an eminent heart surgeon, and for that, he deserves considerable respect. And yet I can feel myself looking at him differently.'

'I know that feeling,' I said, thinking of the way my feelings for Nathan seemed to have suddenly changed. 'But are you saying you think you love him a little less?'

She shrugged. 'Maybe. I don't know. Since we got back together, the minute he touches me I'm usually on fire. Obviously, after the accident, if you can call it that, at Christmas, sex took a bit of a back seat, but just a touch of his hand sent the same wonderful sensations rushing through me. The last couple of days, it's taken a little longer for the flames to ignite. I do still want him, and sex with him is still fantastic, but now I've found myself wondering if, to him, sex is just something he needs, and that's sort of taken a bit of the romance out of it for me. People can be sex addicts, can't they? And if that is Alex's problem, I can't help but wonder if, in spite of what he says, he may start wandering again.'

'Surely the fact that one of his 'women' tried to mow you down with a car and got him instead has shown him the error of his ways?' Josie said, not completely managing to hide her contempt for the way Alex treated people. 'I'd imagine that whole episode gave him serious pause for thought, and he'd already told you he intended to mend his ways. As a doctor, he would know who to turn to if he does need help with an addiction. Have you discussed this with him?'

'No. Not yet. I wanted to analyse my own feelings first. I know I've got to though, or all the work we've started to do to improve our marriage will be wasted.'

'Why are relationships so hard?' I asked.

'They shouldn't be,' Josie said. 'But I think everyone has problems. I'm not sure there's such a thing as the perfect relationship.' She grinned broadly. 'But mine and Liam's comes pretty close.'

'It's early days,' Diana said, with a smile. 'Let's see how you feel after sixteen years of marriage. Although I do think you and Liam were made for one another.'

'So do I,' Josie agreed. 'And Lottie and Asher were too.'

Lottie beamed at her. 'I think we were. Some people say that we're all only half the person we could be and that our other half is out there searching. It's only when you meet that other half that you become whole. I genuinely feel that way about Asher. He completes me and I believe I complete him.'

'Aww,' I said. 'That's so sweet. And I think it's true. Asher does seem more content since meeting you. I'm not saying he wasn't happy with his life before then, but he was always on the go, rushing here and there, keeping busy. Now he's much more relaxed somehow. That bit you said about searching makes sense. It's as if he was missing something and he's found it with you.'

'I'll go along with that,' Josie said. 'I thought I was happy until Liam showed me what real happiness is.'

'Hmm,' said Diana. 'I'm not sure where that leaves me and Alex. But I don't think I want to be without him. I tried that and when it came to it, I wanted him back. For better or worse, I suppose.'

We walked on in silence for a second or two, Merry and Henry snuffling the ground like truffle-hunting hounds, which neither of them were.

'There must be something wrong with me,' I said, kicking a pile of wet leaves and then feeling guilty in case some little woodland creatures had made the pile their home. Thankfully, I couldn't see anything, living or dead when I stopped to look.

'Have you dropped something?' Diana asked.

'No. I thought I might've killed something, or made it homeless, but I don't think I did.'

'Why do you think there's something wrong with you?' Josie queried, grinning at me as we continued on.

'Because I keep falling in love with the wrong people, but now, when I've finally fallen for the right guy, I may be about to mess it up. I know I'm in love with Finlay, and although it was all very sudden, everyone agrees that this time I seem to have made the right choice. Even Mum and Dad think he's perfect and I know you all thought he was nice when you met him at the party. And yet I can't seem to get ... someone else out of my head.'

'Someone else?' Diana and Josie exchanged glances and Lottie stared at the ground.

'And who's that, may we ask?' Josie stared at me, still grinning all the while. 'You can't leave us wondering.'

'Lottie clearly knows,' Diana said. 'You've got to tell us, Sorcha. You can't keep it a secret.

Is it someone in Seahorse Harbour?'

I nodded. 'I'm not trying to keep it a secret. I just can't believe it's happening. And I don't want it to be.'

'Is he married or something?' Diana's smile faded a smidgeon.

'No. Nothing like that.'

'It had better not be Liam,' Josie laughed. 'Is it Mikkel?'

Diana glared at her, not looking happy at the prospect that it might be. Even though her own affair with Mikkel had been over for a while now, she had told us all that, as selfish as it was, she didn't like the thought of him being with anyone else.

'No. It's ... It's Nathan Bromley.'

'Nathan?' Diana and Josie said in unison.

'That's excellent news.' Josie seemed thrilled.

'Why is that a problem?' Diana asked.

I sighed heavily. 'Because I've never seen Nathan as anything other than a friend, and sometimes not even that, but since last night, all I can think about, all I can picture in my head, is him. And him and me doing things together that I *really* never thought I'd want to do with Nathan Bromley.'

'What happened last night?' Josie shrieked.

I forgot they didn't know so I filled them in about everything, including the arrangement to meet Finlay in the hotel and then cancelling after the bathroom incident. They listened intently, oohing and ahhing at various stages and giving Lottie sideways glances as if she might know more juicy details.

'Hmm,' Josie said when I had finished. 'Perhaps all this time you've slowly been falling in love with Nathan but you only realised it last night.'

A burst of almost hysterical laughter escaped me.

'What? And seeing him naked was the catalyst? I was thinking more along the lines of what Diana said about Alex. Maybe I'm sex mad or something, and seeing his rather spectacular body simply made me lust after him.'

They all laughed at that, including Lottie who said, 'Or perhaps Josie's right. Perhaps you finally see him in the same light as the rest of us do. He's a handsome man. Not drop-dead gorgeous, but definitely good-looking. And it's not just his looks. He's also kind, caring and thoughtful. He's the complete package.'

I giggled. 'His package is definitely complete. I got an eyeful last night.'

Lottie tutted, Diana actually blushed.

Josie roared with laughter. 'I wouldn't mind getting an eyeful of his package. Especially if he was wearing that yellow apron beforehand.'

'I'm being serious,' Lottie said.

I fluttered my eyelashes and waved one hand in front of my face. 'So am I.'

Josie nudged me with her elbow. 'So you're telling us that the sight of Nathan's bits made you realise you've fallen in love with him?'

'Not love. Lust. Although last night I did think it might be love. But how can I be in love with a man I dislike? Okay. Maybe not dislike. But a man I clash with every time we're together. I can't, can I? So it must be lust. But what I don't understand, and can't really deal with, is the fact that ever since last night I can't stop thinking about him. Even when I start thinking about being at the hotel with Finlay, it's Nathan's face that pops into my head. What's that all about?'

'I'm sorry to have to say this,' Josie said, 'because I know it's not what you want to hear, but what Lottie and I said, stands. I think you're in love with Nathan, whether you like it or not.'

'But I can't be. I just can't.'

'Why on earth not?' Diana sounded like one of my old schoolteachers, at that moment. 'Nathan's lovely. He's a really decent guy. What's so wrong with being in love with him?'

'Just one teensy-weensy little thing. The guy is *not* in love with me!' I shouted that last part so loudly that I scared a flock of sparrows from the trees and their flapping wings and twittering seemed to be mocking me as I lowered my tone an octave or two. 'I can't fall in love with yet another guy who is just going to break my heart. Finlay loves me. Nathan doesn't.'

'How do you know he doesn't?' Josie nudged me again.

I blinked several times. Was she insane?

'Er. Planet Earth to whichever planet you're currently living on. If Nathan loved me, don't you think he would've done something about it? Like asked me on a date or something? All he does is lecture me, remind me that I fall in love with the wrong men as frequently as the sun rises and sets, and argues with me.'

'Perhaps that's because he's jealous,' she said, stopping suddenly and patting the trunk of a large Copper Beech tree. 'Liam and I were like that. Until we had sex against this very tree. In a thunderstorm.' She positively glowed from the memory.

'You rowed after that,' Diana said, in a matter-of-fact tone.

Josie sneered at her. 'Thanks for reminding me.' She rolled her eyes and laughed. 'It's true. We did.' She patted the tree again. 'But that was the moment we both realised how we felt about one another. We just didn't tell each other until a few weeks later.'

'Maybe that's the issue.' Diana looked

thoughtful. 'Perhaps Nathan thinks you're not interested in him. That's why he hasn't said anything.'

'Or perhaps he doesn't find me attractive. Or I'm not the type of girl he wants to date. As I said, he's always lecturing me about falling for the wrong men. Perhaps that's his way of tactfully saying he thinks I'm a tart. Not that he's very tactful.'

'I don't think that's the case at all,' Lottie said. 'You've mentioned that more than once he's said something along the lines of, "if you were my girlfriend". Doesn't that indicate that he would date you?'

We all stared at her and contemplated what she'd said.

'No,' I said. 'I don't think so. Does it?'

'There's one way to find out.' The grin on Josie's face was huge. 'We could go to Seahorse Bites Café right now and ask him.'

Twenty-One

There was no way in the world that I was going to ask Nathan Bromley straight out if he would ever consider dating me. Or let anyone else ask him for me. But after further discussion all four of us agreed there was no harm in going to the café and seeing how he behaved towards me, and trying to get an indication as to whether or not he had experienced any similar revelations to mine last night.

I don't think I've ever been so nervous in my life.

The more they all agreed that they thought I'd been slowly falling in love with Nathan, the more it seemed to make sense. Except I'd never, ever fallen in love with any man, *slowly* in my life. With me it was always *ker-pow*. Instantaneous, or at least within a day. I had never been friends with someone prior to dating them. I just wasn't made that way. So how could I have slowly drifted into being in love with Nathan Bromley?

And yet, since Nathan had moved to Seahorse Harbour in early January, I did always head down to the beach on the three occasions I had come to stay with Asher.

And during the previous times when Nathan had come to visit Lyn and I'd been at Asher's, I'd always made a point of going to say hello to him, even though the very first time we met, several years ago now, we argued.

I can't recall what it was about but I remember telling Asher that Lyn's nephew was an obnoxious git and I hoped he didn't intend to visit her often because I'd never go to Seahorse Bites Café again if he was there.

But the very next time he visited her, I had made a beeline for the café.

And we had argued again.

Either I was a glutton for punishment and actually enjoyed arguing with him, or I was attracted to him and didn't even know it.

During the years I was married, I hadn't seen Nathan. I hadn't seen anyone and I hadn't visited Asher. My bastard of a husband wouldn't allow it. He wouldn't allow me out of the house in the end. Until Asher came and got me.

The controlling behaviour hadn't happened overnight. When I first met him, I thought he was kind and gentle and caring. A bit too caring perhaps, but I didn't see any warning signs. Other people did, but by then it was already far too late.

Even Nathan warned me against him, so we argued about that. I think that might've been the last time I saw Nathan until my marriage was over.

And yet my ex-husband and I had never actually argued. He simply bullied me into submission.

At first, he just bullied me emotionally, but in the end, he became physically violent too. Thankfully that didn't last for long. I may be incapable of stopping myself from falling for the wrong men, and I may have been foolish in not seeing the signs, but being beaten up soon brought me to my senses, even though I was definitely scared of leaving and being on my own.

I couldn't get out of the house but I did find a way to get a message to Asher, via a neighbour, during one of the rare moments my ex took his eyes off me. He was a graphic designer and he worked from home so he watched me day and night.

Asher came and saved me as soon as he got the message. And I do mean saved me. My ex had completely lost it and if Asher hadn't turned up when he did, I'm not sure I'd be here now.

And yet it didn't put me off men, or falling in love.

And arguing with Nathan never, ever

frightened me. He made me cross, which was a luxury in itself. I hadn't been able to get cross with my ex. At least, I hadn't been able to show it. I felt completely safe with Nathan. I somehow always had.

I was lucky in so many ways. And as awful as this sounds, I was really lucky when my ex had a car crash and died.

That's a dreadful thing to say, but it's true. I'm not sure he would've stayed away from me, despite the court order and the various charges brought against him.

But that's all in the dim and distant past. I do still very occasionally have a nightmare about him, but it doesn't worry me once I'm awake, because I know he isn't around to hurt me.

And no one will ever hurt me like that again.

I may pick all the wrong men, but none of the others has ever shown even the slightest tendency towards violence, or even bullying.

And certainly not Nathan Bromley.

A feeling of panic set in when we walked into the café and I couldn't see any sign of Nathan.

'Hello girls.' Lyn, who was wearing her bright yellow apron, beamed at us as the bell tinkled over the front door. 'Isn't it a lovely day? I'll be with you in just a jiffy. And hello to you, beautiful Merry and handsome Henry.'

Merry and Henry headed directly to the bowls of fresh water Lyn provided for thirsty dogs. There was a row of colourful bowls just to one side of the door.

In the summer months, Lyn put bowls outside too, but in this weather the water froze, or quickly filled up with debris or sand blown in from the streets and the beach, so she kept the bowls inside.

Any dog owner was welcome to pop in for their dog to have a drink though, regardless of whether or not the human bought a beverage or anything for themselves.

'Are you on your own today, Lyn?' Josie asked, sounding casually interested as we sat at a table in the window while Lyn finished wiping down the counter.

'No, love. Nathan's just nipped next door to Bev's to pick up some more fresh bread. We've had a run on bacon butties, sausage sandwiches, and anything and everything on toast today. But one of Bev's ovens is playing up so he's mending it for her.'

'He mends ovens too?' Josie queried, grinning at me. 'He's a man of many talents, isn't he?'

'He is that. And I'm not just saying so because I love him to the moon and back and I'm biased. He's the best man I know. Mark my words, the lucky lady who wins his heart will have riches beyond compare. Providing she's smart enough to see it.'

She threw me an odd look, almost as if she knew I might have fallen in love with her nephew and she was telling me I would never be worthy.

'Has he shown any interest in anyone in Seahorse Harbour?'

Now Lyn looked askance at Josie.

'Why the sudden interest in my nephew, Josie Parnell? You're head over heels in love with Liam.'

'Just curious.'

Josie managed to maintain a friendly smile as if she really was just passing the time of day with Lyn, and not interrogating her on my behalf.

'You know what curiosity gets you, love.' Lyn smiled as the bell tinkled over the door. 'But here he is now, so you can ask him that in person.'

Nathan shot a look towards our table and frowned.

'Ask me what?'

'Josie wants to know if you've got your eye on anyone in the village.'

He looked from Lyn to us and the expression on his face was akin to one of horror.

'Does she?' he eventually said, walking towards the kitchen. 'Sorry, Josie. I don't discuss my personal life.'

'Oh come on, Nathan,' she teased. 'There must be someone you fancy. Give us a clue.'

'I'll give you a menu and my personal recommendation of what's really good today, but that's it.'

His tone was light-hearted and yet his jaw was tense and his gaze was fixed, as if he were struggling to keep his emotions in check. He placed the bread he'd been carrying under his arm, on the counter, picked up four menus and brought them to our table.

'We'll just have to guess then.'

Josie wasn't going to give up and I dreaded to think what she might say next.

'Knock yourself out.' He handed us the menus without glancing once in my direction. 'But you're wasting your time.'

I watched the fluid movement of his body as he turned and walked away and I couldn't help remembering how it had felt last night, when I was standing so close to him.

'What about Sorcha?'

Nathan stopped in his tracks and I nearly died on the spot. I know I gasped but I'm not sure how loudly.

'What about her?' He turned slowly. 'There wouldn't be much point, would there?' He still didn't look at me even though I was staring agog at him. 'She's made it abundantly clear how she feels about me. And besides, I think you'll find she believes she's in love with someone else.'

That made me cross.

'I am right here you know!' I hissed.

'I'm well aware of that.'

'Then what's with the 'she'?'

'I was merely answering a question.'

'Really? That's it?' I jumped to my feet. 'Well for your information, Mr Know It All, you have no idea how I feel about you. Not a clue. And don't presume to know who I am or am not in love with. Because it just so happens I...'

I managed to stop myself just in time. Everyone was looking at me and even the dogs were wide-eyed and attentive.

'Yes, love?' Lyn coaxed. 'It just so happens you what?'

'Er.' I darted a look at Josie and the others, hoping one of them would get me out of the hole I'd dug myself into, but all three of them continued staring at me in both surprise and anticipation. 'Er. Because I believe it's none of anyone's business who I love.' I dropped back down on the seat and lowered my gaze to the table.

A moment of awkward silence ensued before Nathan turned and walked away without another word.

'Well that's a turn up for the books,' Lyn said, smiling oddly, both at Nathan's retreating back and then at my burning cheeks. 'Now what can I get you all? The lemon drizzle cake is scrumptious.'

Twenty-Two

I didn't see Nathan again that day. He remained in the kitchen and clearly didn't want to come out because it was Lyn who brought us our two hot chocolates, two pots of tea, and four slices of lemon drizzle cake.

We only stayed for the amount of time it took us to eat and drink, which was about twenty minutes in total but even when Josie shouted out a goodbye to Nathan, all he did was shout a goodbye back.

The oddest part was that none of us said anything about what had happened. Not Lyn, and not even Josie until the four of us had left the café.

'I think we got our answer,' Josie said, beaming at me as we walked up Church Hill.

'Did we?' Lottie clearly hadn't.

'Yes,' Diana said. 'Isn't it obvious?'

'Yes,' I said. 'He's not interested in me. He couldn't even be bothered saying my name. He just called me 'she'. The bloody moron.'

Josie stopped and grabbed me by the shoulders, shaking me, but in a playful manner.

'What is wrong with you, woman? Nathan is clearly crazy about you.'

'No he isn't. He didn't even say he liked me as a friend. He didn't say how he felt about me at all.'

'Precisely. But what he did say was that you weren't interested in him and that you believe you're in love with someone else. Don't you see? It's exactly as we thought. He loves you but he thinks you believe you love someone else and that you wouldn't look at him even if that weren't the case.'

'I agree,' Diana said.

'I'm not sure,' said Lottie. 'But yes. That does make sense.'

'Not to me it doesn't.'

I had no idea what they were saying.

Josie tutted and rolled her eyes. 'All you've got to do, Sorcha, is summon up the courage to tell him how you feel and you'll see we're right.'

'Oh, is that all? Well fine. I'll just nip back right now and say, 'Hey Nathan. I just want you to know that I think I'm in love with you.' Is that what you want me to do?'

'Not quite like that.' Josie shook her head and laughed. 'But something along those lines, yeah.'

'Not going to happen. Sorry. I've made a

big enough fool of myself today, thanks.'

'Someone's got to make the first move,' Diana said. 'I don't think it's going to be Nathan. And certainly not while he thinks you're in love with Finlay.'

'But now I'm not sure I am in love with ... oh my God! I've done it again. I was supposed to be meeting Finlay at the hotel today. He called first thing this morning and asked me to meet him after lunch. It's his last day here before he and his friends go back to London and he wanted to meet me so that we could make plans for the future. And have sex, of course. I said I'd be there at 2.30 and it's almost 3 p.m. now. I've got to go.'

'Why?' Lottie queried. 'If you've decided you don't love him and you love Nathan, why are you going to meet Finlay?'

'Because he's waiting for me and I need to tell him I'm not sure how I feel now.'

'That's what these are for.' Josie waggled her phone in the air as it rang and she answered Liam's call. 'Hi Liam. Can I call you back? Bit of a girlie emergency here. Love you. Bye.'

'I can't tell him over the phone.' The thought hadn't occurred to me for a second. 'We were in love, however briefly, and you don't end a relationship with a phone call.'

Josie shrugged. 'It was hardly a relationship, was it? But suit yourself. It's probably not a bad idea because if you see

Finlay again and it's still Nathan you want to be with, then you'll know for sure that what you feel for Nathan really is love. But if you get there and are even slightly tempted to have sex with Finlay, then it's not. Because why would you want to have sex with someone when you're in love with someone else?'

Diana sighed. 'That's a question I've asked Alex more times than I can remember. And I had an affair with Mikkel even though I still loved Alex. Sorry. That isn't helpful is it?'

'No,' Josie said. 'It isn't.'

'I wouldn't.' I knew myself well enough to know that. 'So you're right. This will tell me once and for all if I love Nathan. Because Finlay is sooooo gorgeous and if I can be in a hotel room with a man as hot as that and not do anything, I'm definitely in love with Nathan.'

'If you do tell Nathan how you feel,' Lottie said. 'You might want to forget that bit. No man wants to hear that you realised you loved them because you didn't have sex in a hotel room with a man far more gorgeous than him.'

'Good point. Right. I'd better grab a cab and get to the hotel. Wish me luck.'

I dialled the local cab company and, while the others waited with me, I texted Finlay to tell him I was running a little late and that I needed to talk to him.

I was a bit distressed when Asher's friend Jonno drove up. Of all the cab drivers, it had to be him. Then again, he was the only cab driver who lived in Seahorse Harbour so even though the cab company was based in Easterhill, the chances of it being him were actually rather high.

I made some excuse about having a spa treatment booked and Jonno didn't question it. There was no reason why he should. He did ask why the others hadn't come with me though and it took me a few seconds to think of a reply.

'It was a Christmas present but I forgot about it until now and the spa only had space for one.'

I'm not sure he believed me but he didn't question it.

We chatted about the engagement party and I asked if he'd known Tiny long.

'Not really. I met him a few times when he wanted a cab from Easterhill station to his gran's, and we always had a chat. Mainly about football. But when he inherited the cottage, he asked me if I could do a bit of work around the place. I'd mentioned that as well as driving my cab, I was a handyman. That's when we became mates. That was about three and a half years ago.'

'Do you know Finlay, Andy and the others too?'

I was hoping to get some info, even though I knew I wasn't going to have a future with Finlay now.

Jonno shook his head. 'Nope. Never met any of them until the party on Friday. I think a couple of them came down last year, because Tiny invited me to meet up with him and some of his mates for a pint and a curry one Friday night around the end of October. But Sandra and I were on holiday in Tenerife for the last two weeks of October, and they were gone by the time we got back. I don't know why I remember that so clearly, but I do. Oh, Jesus. Wasn't that the same time as you had that episode with that conman?' He shot a look at me via the rear view mirror and smiled sympathetically.

I nodded and smiled back even though the memory certainly wasn't a happy one.

'Yes. But let's not talk about that.'

'Right you are. Sorry, Sorcha. Asher did tell me you were all trying to put that stuff behind you. I'll shut up. And I think that's what's called perfect timing.'

He turned from the main road onto the long, tree-lined drive of the Easterhill Hotel and Spa and pulled up right outside the front door of the hotel.

I was only about forty minutes later than I should've been, but I'd already texted Finlay and told him I would be, so I knew he wouldn't be cross.

After paying Jonno, and asking him to say hello to his lovely wife, Sandra, for me, I raced inside and took the lift to the room, Finlay having texted me the number.

I tapped on the door and when he opened it, for just a fraction of a second, I was excited to see him but when he pulled me into his arms, Nathan's face popped into my head and I eased myself away.

'I'm really sorry about this Finlay – and this time I insist on paying half the cost of the room – but I'm afraid we need to talk.'

His entire body tensed and a flash of something akin to anger … or more like, fear, which was odd, flashed across his eyes.

'I'm not sure I like the sound of that.'

I scanned the room for a place to sit and walked towards the chair but he took my hands in his and led me to the bed.

'It's more comfortable if we both sit here,' he said.

I hesitated for a moment but then thought what the hell. We were both fully dressed and I for one intended to make sure we stayed that way.

'I did fall for you the minute I saw you,' I said, once we sat down.

'And I felt the same.' He leaned forward, placing one hand behind my head.

I moved away. 'Please don't, Finlay. I need you to listen to what I have to say.'

That same look appeared again and I began to feel uneasy. When it came right down to it, I was in a hotel room with a man I knew very little about. Almost nothing, in fact.

Why did I always seem to get myself into situations like this? Situations that Asher often had to get me out of.

I really was an idiot. Everyone was right. What would Nathan say if he knew where I was right now? I had to get this over with. And fast.

'O-ka-y,' he said, eyeing me beneath furrowed brows.

'There's no easy way to say this,' I continued. 'The thing is, I've discovered I'm in love with someone else.'

A burst of sarcastic laughter escaped from him and took me completely by surprise but a moment later he looked as if his heart was breaking.

'I didn't expect that. I'm sorry.' He ran a hand through his blond hair and took a deep breath and it was as if he was another person. 'Don't do this to me, Sorcha. Please. I love you.'

'I'm sorry, Finlay. I really am. I didn't want this to happen, believe me. It was the last thing I expected. But I can't change the way I feel.'

'But you have changed the way you feel. On Friday you said you loved me. You said the same on Saturday and on Sunday too.'

'I thought I did.'

'But now you're telling me you don't? What's made you change your mind? Was it something I said? Or didn't say? Was it because

I didn't kiss you on Saturday? Damn it. I knew I should've kissed you.'

'No. It wouldn't have made any difference. At least I don't think it would've. This has nothing to do with you. It's not because of anything you've said or done, or haven't said or done. It's because of something that someone else has said and done. No. Actually it's not. Not really. It's because of me. It's because I think I've finally figured out who and what I want. Although he doesn't feel the same, I don't think.'

'Who? Who is it? You're not making much sense. Is it that guy from the café? I thought there was something between the two of you.'

'Yes. But there's nothing going on with us. I love him. I'm not sure how he feels about me. But that's not really the point and it doesn't matter who it is. What matters is that I realised I don't love you. I thought I might love you both. But I don't. I'm sorry, Finlay. Really I am.'

'Then why did you come here? Maybe, deep down, you do still love me. Maybe you're having doubts.'

I shook my head. 'No. I came here because I felt I owed you an explanation, face to face. And because I think I did fall for you on Friday. However briefly.'

'Then ... can't we have just this one afternoon and evening together? I want you so badly, it physically hurts.' He took my hands again and pulled me to him. 'Just once. Please. So that I can remember this.'

It sounded like a line from a particularly bad movie and I yanked my hands away.

'No, Finlay. I didn't come here to have sex with you. I came here to say I'm sorry.'

I stood up to leave but he grabbed my arm.

'Don't go. Not like this. I'm sorry, Sorcha. It's just that ... well, I came here feeling like I'd found the answer to all my prayers and now ... it feels as if I'm about to lose everything.'

He relaxed his hold but didn't remove his hand until I glared at his fingers.

No man other than my ex-husband had ever been violent towards me, and even though Finlay had grabbed my arm, I wasn't exactly frightened.

'I didn't mean to hurt you, Finlay. You must believe that. I know it's no consolation but if things had worked out differently, we probably would've spent at least one night together by now. Or maybe not. I don't know. I'm still a little confused by this whole thing. I am truly sorry though.'

'Let's have a drink?' He brightened suddenly. 'To friendship. To love. And to what might have been. Just one quick drink. I got us a bottle of champagne. I thought we would be celebrating. I can't sit here and drink it by myself but I'd rather not let it go to waste. Please, Sorcha. Don't you feel you can at least give me that?'

He smiled at me and the puppy-dog look in his eyes won me over.

'Okay. Yes. Just one quick drink. And then I must go.'

Twenty-Three

My head was pounding and my throat felt as if a porcupine had used it for a race track. I opened my eyes and the room swam as twilight crept in through the window. Only it wasn't the window in my room in Asher's cottage as I'd expected. It was the room at the Easterhill Hotel and I was lying in the bed wearing nothing but my underwear.

In spite of my headache, I sat bolt upright.

And that's when I saw him.

Finlay was sitting in the chair opposite; dressed but with his shirt undone and hanging loose outside his trousers.

Horror swept through me and I wanted to scream but I couldn't seem to find my voice.

'You're awake!' He sounded relieved as he hurried towards me. 'Christ. I was beginning to think you'd never wake up. Please don't get upset. Please don't scream. It's not what you think. Nothing happened, I swear.'

Finally I found my voice as I yanked the

covers over my body and up to my neck.

'We didn't? ... You didn't? ... What happened? Where are my clothes?'

'No. We didn't. Nothing happened. Your clothes are right there.' His voice was heavy with remorse as he pointed towards the dressing table stool. 'But I do need to tell you something and you're not going to like what you hear. You should drink plenty of water first.'

'What? What are you saying? I don't understand. Why does my throat feel so awful?'

He sighed loudly. 'That's probably because of the drug I put in your drink yesterday.'

'Drug! Yesterday!' I hurt my throat more by screeching. 'What drug? What the hell are you saying? Are you telling me it's now Tuesday morning? What did you do to me?'

I scrambled to get out of the bed but he was in front of me and holding me tightly.

'Stay calm, Sorcha. I can explain everything but I need you to stay calm.'

'Stay calm? Let me go or I'll scream.'

I went to do so but he clamped one hand over my mouth.

'Please don't. Please just listen. I didn't do anything other than undress you. And slip something in your drink before that. But other than that, I did nothing. Not a thing. And I'm not going to do anything to you now. You're safe. You have my word. But I need you to hear me out. Now I'm going to let go of you and back away, okay? Please don't scream. I can promise you that as soon as I've explained, I'm going to go to the police. Just give me five minutes. You need to hear what I have to say.'

He did as he said and slowly backed away from me, his eyes anxious, his expression filled with shame and remorse.

'The police! Oh my God. What is going on?'

He picked up my clothes and slowly passed them to me, holding them out from a distance as if he thought I might shout, or scream, or lash out if he moved closer again. He behaved as though I were a wild animal that he was trying to placate.

I grabbed them and quickly slid into my jeans and jumper, beneath the covers, while staring at him the entire time in case he did move closer.

'I'm not sure where to start, so I'll start with what happened yesterday.' He took a long breath and sat on the chair. 'After you said you weren't going to stay, I spiked your drink. Don't ask questions yet, please.' He held up one hand in a stop gesture. 'I'll fill in the details later. Let me just get this out. It only took a few minutes for the drug to start to take hold. I've never used anything like that before – and I never will again – but I didn't know how it worked, or how long it would take, or when you would wake up afterwards, when the effects wore off.

When I was sure you were out of it, I ... I undressed you.'

I gasped even though I knew he must've done that, and I tried to take in what he was telling me.

'You were supposed to be completely naked, but I ... I couldn't do it.'

He hung his head low and his fingers twisted as if he were holding knitting needles between them.

'Couldn't do what?' I croaked out the words. 'Couldn't...?'

I couldn't bring myself to say it. It was too horrific to bear. I suddenly started shaking and panic gnawed its way into the pit of my stomach.

He shook his head. It was a slow and almost desperate gesture. He gradually raised his eyes to meet mine.

'This isn't what you imagine. It isn't what you believe it to be. If you'd come to bed with me willingly, yes, I would've slept with you, but when you said you didn't want to, sex was never my intention. I swear I didn't touch you in any way other than to remove your jeans and jumper. All I was going to do was to take some photos. But I couldn't do it. Because believe it or not, I genuinely do care about you. So I couldn't hurt you.'

'Hurt me? Photos? I ... I don't understand. Finlay! Tell me! What *is* going on?'

He let out such a long sigh that for some reason it reminded me of a party balloon deflating. My emotions were all over the place. One second I felt a touch of rising panic, the next I wanted to hear him out.

'Do you remember Halloween?' He tutted and shook his head again. 'Of course you remember Halloween. What am I saying?' Another sigh. This time shorter. 'The guy you met at Halloween – the guy you fell in love with at the Seahorse Harbour Holiday Park is a mate of mine.'

I almost fell off the bed onto the floor.

'A ... a mate of yours? I ... I don't understand. How can he...? I mean, what has that...?'

I had no idea what I was saying.

'Actually, that's not really true. He's not a mate. He's just someone I happen to know very well. But we're not friends. We're probably the opposite of that.'

'Finlay! You're not making any sense. What's going on?'

'I'll tell you what's going on. Do you remember in the pub that day when I told you why I didn't get drunk? That I'd done something stupid and that I was still paying the price.'

'Yes. But I don't see–'

'Well, this is the price. *You* are the price.'

'What?'

Even though I was now fully clothed, I pulled the covers up to my neck. I glanced towards the door but he was seated in the way of any escape I might try to make. And oddly enough, I did believe he wasn't going to hurt me physically.

'And that phone call in the café,' he said. 'That was Don asking me if I'd done it yet. That's why I was so upset by it.'

'Done what, exactly? This still isn't making any sense.'

I really had no clue what I was saying or what was going on.

'This weekend was all an act. That's what I do. I don't work for an insurance company – although I did. For many years. I still do, I suppose, from time to time, when I need money. But I'm an actor. Not a household name, but I get by. I do the insurance work between gigs.'

'What ... what are you saying? I don't believe you. Are you saying you've made this all up? That you ... that you were never in love with me? Finlay! What's happening? Is this just an awful joke? Some horrific prank? And what does what happened at Halloween have to do with it? Why were you going to take photos of me? And why naked? Is this ... is this some sort of porno thing?'

'It isn't a prank, Sorcha. It's the bitter truth. Please let me continue to explain. I owe you that.'

I couldn't speak anymore, so I just nodded, my mouth hanging open and my head spinning as I tried to make sense of any of it.

'That time I got drunk,' he continued. 'Really drunk. I got involved with a group of guys who weren't ... let's just say, they weren't the type of people I would normally get involved with. They were into serious gambling. And I mean, *serious gambling*. The sort of gambling that once you get involved, it's a bit like being in the Mafia or something. It's almost impossible to get out. Especially when you lose a lot of money to them, as I did that night I got drunk. That was five years ago and it's taken everything I have, not just financially but emotionally, to get out. Although I've paid my debt in full, financially-speaking, you're never really free unless they decide you are. I was told that if I did this favour this weekend, I wouldn't hear from them again. I thought it would be easy. After all, what harm was there in pretending to be in love with someone who falls in love at the flick of a switch? It was just another acting role. Nothing more.'

I could almost feel the metaphorical dagger being plunged into my heart and the full horror of what was happening finally began to sink in. I let him continue, too stunned to speak.

'But I hadn't given any thought to the fact

that there was a real person involved. A person with real feelings who wasn't acting. And I hadn't taken into account the fact that I might actually like you. I do like you, Sorcha. I like you a lot. I hadn't expected that. To me it was just a gig. But then there was that incident with Alex Dunn. And I couldn't stop thinking about that. About how much I despised the man for not remembering Veronica's name. And it hit me that I was no better than him if I went through with this. In fact, it would make me the scum of the earth, and I couldn't handle that. And why, although I was annoyed that I couldn't pull this off, I was glad that we didn't rush into anything on Friday night, and that you cancelled Saturday. And then, in the café, I got that call. I thought I could perhaps still go through with it, but I held back just in case. That's why I kept making excuses not to kiss you. But he called me again and really put the pressure on and I caved. And when you came here and told me you loved someone else, I thought I could definitely go ahead, so I spiked your drink. Except I couldn't do it. I decided that I'd rather take whatever's coming my way than live with the knowledge that I was worse than Alex Dunn. That's why I can't go through with this. Why I can't hurt you. Why I can't betray your trust.' He made a strange sound – a bit like someone choking as they were being strangled. 'That's a stupid thing to say because

I have hurt you. I have betrayed your trust. I realise that. And I'm so, so sorry. I really am. But you don't know these guys, Sorcha. They've never killed anyone – as far as I know, but they can make sure you don't look good for some time. I depend on my looks for work. That's a pathetic excuse.' He sighed deeply. 'So I know what I have to do now. I have to go to the police. After all, what they asked me to do was blackmail. And possibly worse. And they were going to post all the photos I took of you, all over the internet. That must be some sort of criminal offence, but I have no idea what. They need to be stopped. That much I do know. And I'll do everything I can to help with that.'

'You're telling me that Don, the guy who tried to con me out of my savings, is someone you know and that he's part of some gang or something. He knew you were coming here, to this village and he asked you to pretend to be in love with me at first sight, to get me into bed and to then take photos of me naked which he would post everywhere to ... to what? To humiliate me? To blackmail me and if I didn't pay up the photos would go viral? This is unbelievable. How did he even know I'd be in Seahorse Harbour this weekend?'

'Because he's been keeping tabs on you. You're lucky you're a girl. They have some weird code where they won't use violence against a girl. But they will use any other means to repay a score. I am surprised he didn't arrange to have your brother beaten up, especially as you and Asher had reported the scam at Halloween to the police. But I suppose they thought this would hurt you both far more in the long run. My mates and I were supposed to be having Andy's bachelor do in London but I was asked to arrange it so that we would come down here for the weekend instead and that I would 'meet' you. My mates were up for a break at the seaside, so that part wasn't hard. And as Tiny has a place in Easterhill, when I suggested Seahorse Harbour Holiday Park, which I'd been told to do, they agreed without hesitation. It was a pure fluke that your friend, Jonno asked Tiny to do the disco at your brother's engagement party. I thought we'd lucked out.'

'You ... you didn't take any photos? None at all? And you didn't ... you didn't do anything else?'

He gave another strange little laugh. 'No Photos. Nothing. And no. I swear. I couldn't even bring myself to undress you fully. How crazy is that? I kept telling myself I could do it and to give myself time. But it felt so wrong. So sordid. So bloody awful that I just couldn't go through with it. You'll probably find this hard to believe now, but I'm not that kind of guy. I've never done anything like this before, and you have my word I'll never do anything like it again. No matter what. I've learned a valuable lesson here. Although I know that doesn't make you feel better.'

I felt dirty and horrified and as if I were living in a fantasy of some sort. I didn't know what would happen next. Finlay had said he was going to the police. I supposed that meant they would eventually contact me. They'd taken my statement after the Halloween debacle, so I assumed they'd do the same now. I didn't question whether Finlay would actually go to them or not. I somehow believed he would. All I wanted to do was get out of there as quickly as possible, go home and spend at least an hour in the shower.

I think a small part of me hoped and prayed that I would wake up and find myself in bed at the cottage and discover that this had all been some truly dreadful nightmare.

Sadly though, it wasn't.

Twenty-Four

Asher was furious and wanted to kill Finlay – and everyone else involved. At first I'd considered not telling him about it, but I knew I had to, especially if Finlay did go to the police. They would no doubt want to interview me.

Besides, I needed to confide in Asher. Partly because of what Finlay had said about Don and the fact that the man wanted revenge. As the plan with Finlay had failed, they might now come after Asher and me, in other ways. And maybe even Lottie, although she had nothing to do with it.

The police assured us that wouldn't happen. They also told us that there was an ongoing undercover operation and that charges were imminent. We wouldn't need to worry about Don or any of his gang for many, many years. It wasn't just gambling the man was involved with, but they wouldn't give us any other details, just an emergency number for us to call if we ever felt we needed to.

I felt traumatised in a way. It was as if I was walking around half asleep and no matter how hard I tried, I couldn't wake up fully.

The weirdest part of it all was that I wanted to tell Nathan everything, but I couldn't. I felt so ridiculously guilty for some reason.

Lottie told me that while I was at the hotel with Finlay, Nathan had called at the cottage to have a word with me. She'd told him I'd gone to see a friend and would be back in a couple of hours.

He'd come back that evening, and of course I still wasn't there, thanks to Finlay drugging me.

Lottie, and everyone else who knew about the rendezvous with Finlay had assumed I'd decided to stay and have sex with him after all. It didn't occur to them to call me and check.

But why would they? We all trusted Finlay. And everyone knew I fell in and out of love at the drop of a smile. They assumed Finlay had smiled at me and I'd decided I still loved him, or at the very least, decided I might as well have sex with him.

And even stranger still, it turned out that Finlay Demon wasn't even his name.

Which was why, as Asher told me later, there had been no trace of a Finlay Demon when Asher had Googled the name – just to check, the day after the engagement party.

'Not everyone's on social media,' Asher

later said, 'but it did seem odd that no results for the name Finlay Demon showed up, only results for demons and devils.'

Finlay told me in the hotel that his real name was Finian Devlin. And then I realised why I felt I'd known him the moment I saw him. He'd appeared in a TV series I'd watched a few years before. He looked slightly different, and a good six years older, but as soon as he told me his real name, I recognised it.

'The part made me famous – for about five minutes,' he'd told me. 'And that was when I started gambling. I was earning quite a lot and I threw money around like salt on snowy ground. I got in with a bad crowd where drink, drugs and gambling were second nature. And then, because of my increasingly worse and erratic behaviour, I was fired from the series. I went back to my previous job as an insurance claims administrator, working in between getting a few small parts.'

I almost felt sorry for him when he'd told me that, but nothing could excuse what he had tried to do. The lies he'd told, the trust he'd betrayed. Even my family had believed him. I think that hurt me more than anything.

That, and the fact that Nathan saw me return to the cottage after Finlay's explanation. I know that because I spotted him as I got out of the cab I'd got from the hotel. Thankfully this time it wasn't Jonno who drove the cab. I probably would've blurted it all out to him and he would've gone back to the hotel and possibly done something to Finlay. It was still really early so I'm not sure what Nathan was doing or where he was going, but it looked as if he'd been coming to the cottage. He turned and went back the way he'd come after seeing me. He obviously put two and two together and thought I'd spent the night with Finlay. Which I had. But not in the way he thought.

And then, in spite of Lottie, Josie and Diana all telling me I should come clean with Nathan and they were sure he'd understand, I simply couldn't face him.

I'd done nothing wrong but I felt as if I had. I felt dirty and sordid and stupid. Utterly stupid.

And in a strange way, I even thought Nathan would be better off without me.

I still had no idea how he felt about me but if he did care about me before, would he feel the same once he knew how foolish I'd been?

And if he did still like me, didn't he deserve better? He was a decent, caring, thoughtful guy. He deserved a decent, caring, thoughtful woman. Not some silly tart who fell in love with any man the second she saw him and got herself into situations so awful that she'd married a man who beat her up, and then fell for two others which resulted in the police having to be involved. Not to mention the string of other failed relationships I'd had. Like Sean, for example.

That felt as if it had happened a lifetime ago now, but Nathan knew the truth. I had tumbled out of one bed and almost into another, hardly taking a breath in between.

I wasn't really the sort of girl you'd want to take home to meet your mother.

No. Nathan deserved so much better than me. And I wanted him to be happy. He would be happy without me. The last thing he needed was me dragging him down to my level.

I didn't want to see Nathan, or anyone else, and rumours flew around the village for all sorts of reasons.

We managed to keep most of it under wraps. All we did disclose was that someone had tried to scam me – again, and the police were now involved.

We didn't understand what Finlay – or Finian I suppose I should call him, had intended to do once he'd taken the photos and sent them to Don. But he had told the police, and they told us, that the plan was to say he'd accidently sent them to an online site known to host such explicit photos, and then that others had shared them from there.

He planned to tell me that he'd used the site once or twice to look at naked women, much like buying a magazine, but that he'd uploaded my photos by mistake. He assumed either I'd dump him immediately, or we'd continue seeing one another for a time and then he'd eventually say it wasn't working and walk away, leaving me none the wiser as to what he'd really done.

He was supposed to actually upload the sordid photos to the site, in case of any future police involvement, but thankfully, he hadn't taken any, because he'd decided he couldn't go through with it.

The police did confiscate his phone and their specialists carried out a variety of checks. It was true that Finlay hadn't taken any compromising photos of me, but he had taken one photo. It was one of me fully clothed, sitting opposite him in Seahorse Bites Café. He told the police he wanted one photo of me, but that was all he said.

I went home to my parents and licked my wounds, miles away from Seahorse Harbour.

I can honestly say it was the strangest few weeks of my life. Even taking into account my awful marriage and the fall-out from that.

I don't think anything really sank in at the hotel that day with Finlay. I still can't get used to using his real name. But as the police kept us informed and I thought more and more about it all, I put all the pieces of the puzzle in place. And for what it was worth, I do think Finlay genuinely liked me. Not loved me, obviously, but liked me.

I still couldn't believe that I fell for Finlay, or Finian I should say. Although as he was playing a part, I suppose it was his character of Finlay Demon I fell in love with.

Would I have fallen for Finian if he'd been himself and not playing a part?

I'll never know. Possibly, I think.

I'm just so grateful that I realised I was actually in love with Nathan. The timing couldn't have been better.

Destiny, you see.

At least that's what I think it was.

We returned to visit Asher and Lottie on Easter Sunday, when things had started to settle down and the gossip had subsided.

The gossip concerning me, at least. Now the village had something far juicier to whisper about. But I won't go into that now. And besides, I know how painful it can be when you're the one bearing the brunt of gossiping tongues.

I felt both nervous and excited to be back in Seahorse Harbour.

Needless to say, Asher and Lottie welcomed me with open arms, and this time Mum and Dad also stayed at the cottage. That meant me sleeping on the sofa, but I really didn't mind.

Don't ask me why, but I walked down towards the beach the night we arrived. I hadn't meant to and I'm still not sure why I did.

I walked in the other direction at first, but within a matter of minutes, my feet had turned towards the promenade and Seahorse Bites Café.

I think I just wanted to see Nathan again, even from a distance.

I saw the lights were on and as it was Sunday evening, I knew he'd probably be doing the accounts. Even on a Bank Holiday. But as I got closer, I saw that only one light was on and the rest of the café was in darkness.

I stood beside the wall of Beach Bakers and edged my way along, stopping when I reached the façade of the café. I peered into the window hoping Nathan was somewhere inside and that I could see him but he wouldn't see me.

'Looking for anyone in particular?'

I knew it was him the moment I heard the first word and I froze on the spot. Where the hell had he come from?

As if reading my mind he walked around me and stood before me, smiling as if he was actually pleased to see me.

'I've just been to Asher's,' he said, 'But Lottie told me you'd gone for a walk and that you might've come down here. How are you? I'm so glad you've come back.'

'I … I'm fine, thanks. How are you?'

'I'm good. Really good. I've got a lot to tell you.'

'I … I can't stop. Sorry. I must get back. I

said I'd only be a minute.'

I wanted to turn away and run but I also wanted to keep looking at his face, the line of his jaw, the softness of his lips, the sparkle in his eyes and that gorgeous smile. I'd never noticed how wonderful it was.

'Don't go, Sorcha. Please stay. There's something I need to tell you. Something I should've told you a long time ago, I think.'

I stared at him, half hopeful, half terrified. What did he want to tell me? That he was leaving Seahorse Harbour and returning to his life as an architect?

Or was there a chance – just the tiniest chance, that he wanted to tell me he liked me? I knew he didn't love me. How could he? Not after the way I'd behaved. I had acted like a silly little girl, not a grown woman.

'What is it, Nathan?'

It felt wonderful to say his name and to look at him.

'I think there's probably a better way for me to say this, but right now I can't think of one, so I'll just say it, okay? And don't bite my head off. Josie told me that you were coming back today. She also told me what really happened with Finlay. But more importantly, she told me that you loved me. That you had chosen me over Finlay but that you couldn't tell me how you felt. Is that true? Actually, it doesn't matter right now. What matters is that

I love you. I've loved you for years, I think, although I didn't realise that until this January when I came back here. But I do. I love you, Sorcha. With all my heart.'

I blinked at him in silence.

He gave me a nervous sort of smile. 'Okay. Er. It would be good if you responded in some way. Any way at all. Oh God. Have I got this all wrong? Have you changed the way you feel? Have I lost you again?'

'No! No, Nathan. Nothing's changed. Nothing. I do love you. I'm crazy about you. But I'm a mess. I'm a stupid fool.'

He was grinning at me now and his eyes were dancing with emotion. With love.

'And your point is?'

'I'm not the sort of woman you should be with.'

'Shouldn't I be the one to decide that?'

'But I've been such an idiot, Nathan.'

He reached out his hand and brushed my cheek with his fingers.

'You're not an idiot, Sorcha. You're not a mess or a stupid fool. You're beautiful. You're wonderful. You're vulnerable. You're trusting and hopeful. You're the woman I love. You've just been looking for love in all the wrong places. And you know the old saying, "Love comes when you're not looking for it." You definitely weren't looking for love with me.'

I gave a little laugh and pressed my cheek

against his hand, twisting a little so that I could plant a tiny kiss on his fingers.

'I didn't think I was. And to be honest, when I realised I loved you, it took me completely by surprise. But when I finally admitted it to myself, it seemed the most natural thing in the world. Does that make sense?'

'Perfect sense.'

'And you've been in love with me all this time?'

I still couldn't quite believe it. Or understand what I'd done to get so lucky.

He nodded and smiled lovingly.

'I've been in love with you since the first time we met, I think.'

I gasped and pushed myself away from him, laughing as I did.

'Nathan Bromley! Are you telling me you fell in love with me at first sight? Seriously? I didn't think you believed in that.'

He shrugged. 'What can I say?' A huge grin spread across his face. 'Some people are just made for one another. You can't fight Destiny, however hard you might try.'

'Did you try?'

'Several times. Every time I heard you'd fallen in love with someone new I cursed myself for loving you, and told myself I needed to get over you because I didn't stand a chance. But each time I was told you were single again, a flicker of hope ignited and the flames of passion consumed me again.'

'The flames of passion consumed you?' I raised my brows.

He gave me the most delightful – and the sexiest – smile I'd ever seen.

'Love makes us feel, and say, things we usually wouldn't.'

'You told me off every time you saw me. Or gave me a lecture.'

He gently pulled me towards him. 'But all I wanted to do was take you in my arms–'

'And shake some sense into me.' I laughed as I threw his words back at him, excited to be in his arms. To feel them wrapped around me. 'Although what you actually said before was, "take you by your arms". He had never mentioned taking me in his arms. But now that he had, I never wanted him to let me go.

He shook his head. 'And kiss you. I wanted to show you how I felt. To make you see that there was a man who loved you, standing right in front of you. A man who would do his best to never let you down and would do anything he could to make you happy.'

'Why didn't you? Take me in your arms and kiss me, I mean?'

He tipped his head to one side and gave me a look of disbelief.

'Seriously?' His laughter sent tingles from my head to my toes. 'For one thing, you probably would've slapped my face. For another ... I wouldn't have wanted to stop at kissing you, and it would've taken every ounce of self-control not to try to take things further. Do you remember that night in the bathroom at Asher's?'

'How could I forget? You told me to get out.'

'Only because I was fighting the urge to kiss you. And I was naked. Things were getting ... let's just say, things were getting hard to cope with.'

'You wanted to kiss me?'

'Desperately.'

'Do you want to kiss me now?'

'Absolutely.'

He pulled me even closer, and kissed me in a way that I have never been kissed before. And before I lost myself completely in his kiss, I swear I could hear bells ringing, and people singing, and it sounded very much like they were booming out, 'Hallelujah! Hallelujah! Hallelu-u-u-jah!'

I realised they were. It was the dulcet tones of the church choir wafting towards us on the evening air. It was late. But they were dedicated. Or perhaps there were special services on Easter Sunday. I hadn't been to church in years. And I didn't really care why they were there.

And as his kiss deepened, I completely

forgot about the choir.

Although it wasn't long before I was yelling, 'Hallelujah!' Or something very similar.

Because I have to tell you, not only was Nathan Bromley an exceptionally good kisser, and so, so much better than all the rest, he was also unbelievably and sensationally good at everything else he did next.

He took my hand and led me inside the café, into the little room at the back where there was a small sofa and a table and he sat me down on the sofa, kissing me all the while.

His hands moved over my body, softly and slowly at first but then with more urgency and intensity and desire and when his lips trailed down to my breast and his fingers explored every inch of me, I clung to him, terrified he'd stop. Or that this was all some fantastic dream.

'Oh God!' I screamed in ecstasy. 'I love you, Nathan.'

He stopped the incredible things he was doing, for just one moment, and looked me in the eye. He held my gaze and his eyes reflected exactly how I felt.

'I love you too, Sorcha. And you can be sure I'll love you till the day I die.'

'Same ... here,' I said, gasping for breath as he resumed what he'd been doing, while also kissing me so deeply I could feel it right down to my toes. And everywhere else in between.

It was as if a part of me had been missing until now.

The best part of me.

I had finally found my other half.

My missing part.

I would never fall in love with any other man. And that realisation made me blissfully happy.

I *had* finally found The One.

And his name was Nathan Bromley.

Coming soon

Dreams and Schemes at The Seahorse Inn

A dream. A scheme. An undeniable attraction.

When Mikkel Meloy discovers Seahorse Harbour Holiday Park together with half of Little Wood, is up for sale, he knows he has to buy it. Mikkel needs a project to take his mind off his recent heartbreak and he's got big plans to transform the rundown caravan park and the tranquil area of woodland into a holiday haven of eco-cabins.

Unfortunately for him, he's not the only one interested in the place, and as the eldest daughter of the owner of the chain of hugely successful Trulove Hotels, Portia Trulove isn't used to anyone getting in her way. Sparks fly the moment Mikkel and Portia meet but neither can deny the instant attraction between them.

Despite Mikkel not being entirely sure he's over Diana Dunn, the woman who recently broke his heart, and Portia making it clear she's not about to fall in love with anyone, it isn't long before those sparks turn into flames and Mikkel and Portia are sharing more than angry words.

But is Portia genuinely interested in Mikkel? Or is this merely a scheme to throw him off balance? Because only one of them can succeed in fulfilling their dreams by getting their hands on the object of their desire – Seahorse Harbour Holiday Park.

And rumour has it that Portia Trulove will do anything to get what she wants.

This is book 5 in my new series of standalone novels set in the tiny, seaside village of Seahorse Harbour.

A Note from Emily

Thank you for reading this book. If you loved it and want to be the first to find out about my new books, and also, chat with me and other fans, ask to join the exclusive Emily Harvale's Readers' Club Facebook group. Or go to: www.emilyharvale.com and subscribe to my newsletter via the 'Sign me up' box.

A little piece of my heart goes into all my books and when I send them on their way, I really hope they bring a smile to someone's face. If this book made you smile, or gave you a few pleasant hours of relaxation, I'd be delighted if you'd tell your friends.
I'd also love it if you have a minute or two to post a review. Just a few words will do, and a kind review makes such a difference to my day – to any author's day. Huge thanks to those of you who do so, and for your lovely comments and support on social media. Thank you.
A writer's life can be lonely at times. Sharing a virtual cup of coffee or a glass of wine, or exchanging a few friendly words on Facebook, Twitter or Instagram is so much fun.

I mentioned my newsletter just now. It's absolutely free, your email address is safe and won't be shared and I won't bombard you, I promise. You can enter competitions and enjoy some giveaways. In addition to that, there's my author page on Facebook and there's also my lovely, Facebook group. You can chat with me and with other fans and get access to my book news, snippets from my daily life, early extracts from my books and lots more besides. Details are on my website but you'll find all my contact links in the Contact section following this.

I'm working on my next book right now. Let's see where my characters take us this time. Hope to chat with you soon. In the meantime, I'm sending you love and virtual hugs. I can't wait to bring you more stories that I hope will capture your heart, mind and imagination, allowing you to escape into a world of romance in some enticingly beautiful settings.

To see details of my other books, please go to the books page on my website, or scan the QR code below to see all my books on Amazon.

Stay in touch with

Emily Harvale

If you want to be one of the first to hear Emily's news, find out about book releases, see covers, and enter free competitions, then sign up to her Readers' Club by visiting:

www.emilyharvale.com

and subscribing to her newsletter via the 'Sign me up' box. If you love Emily's books and want to chat with her and other fans, ask to join the exclusive

Emily Harvale's Readers' Club Facebook group

Or come and say 'Hello' on social media:

 @EmilyHarvaleWriter

 @EmilyHarvale

 @EmilyHarvale

Acknowledgements

My grateful thanks go to the following:

Christina Harkness for her patience and care in editing this book.
My webmaster, David Cleworth who does so much more than website stuff.
My cover design team, JR.
Luke Brabants. Luke is a talented artist and can be found at: www.lukebrabants.com
My wonderful friends for their friendship and love. You know I love you all.
All the fabulous members of my Readers' Club. You help and support me in so many ways and I am truly grateful for your ongoing friendship. I wouldn't be where I am today without you.
My Twitter and Facebook friends, and fans of my Facebook author page. It's great to chat with you. You help to keep me (relatively) sane!

Printed in Great Britain
by Amazon

57992894R00151